Recipe for Trouble

The CUPCAKE CLUB

Sheryl Berk and Carrie Berk

sourcebooks
jabberwocky

Published by Sourcebooks Jabberwocky, an imprint of Sourcebooks, Inc.
P.O. Box 4410, Naperville, Illinois 60567-4410
(630) 961-3900
Fax: (630) 961-2168
www.jabberwockykids.com

Library of Congress Cataloging-in-Publication data is on file with the publisher.

Source of Production: Versa Press, East Peoria, Illinois, USA
Date of Production: April 2013
Run Number: 20113

Printed and bound in the United States of America.
VP 10 9 8 7 6 5 4 3

To Peter, aka "Honey" and "Daddy."
You make every day sweeter and fill our hearts with love.

Summer Surprises

The minute Lexi Poole's laptop sang out "You've got mail!" she dropped her sketchbook and colored pencils, and raced over to her desk to check her messages.

She hoped it was an email from one of her friends saying they'd arrived home from summer break. But no such luck. It was just an ad for a back-to-school supplies sale at New Fairfield Stationery. "Ugh!" she moaned.

Most kids loved summer vacation: sun, fun, and no homework! But Lexi missed Blakely Elementary School. She missed her teachers. She missed art class. And she especially missed Peace, Love, and Cupcakes, the cupcake club that had grown to mean so much to her in fourth grade. It was where she had learned to pipe beautiful designs in frosting and sculpt fancy flowers and figures out of gum paste and chocolate. But most importantly, it was where she had met her three BFFs: Kylie Carson, Jenna Medina, and Sadie Harris.

At first, none of them were eager to join Kylie's baking club—it sounded a little lame. But then, something magical happened. Though they were all very different people, they came together to form an awesome, unbreakable team! In just a few short months, everyone wanted to hire them to bake cupcakes. Mr. Ludwig, owner of the Golden Spoon Gourmet Shop in Greenwich, Connecticut, even placed a weekly order of 300 cupcakes!

But for Lexi, being in the cupcake club wasn't about being popular or even making money. It was about belonging. Just knowing that she had Kylie, Jenna, and Sadie by her side made her feel less shy. No matter what happened, she wasn't alone. Yes, there had been some crazy adventures (like the time their Leaning Tower of Pisa 3,000-cupcake display toppled to the floor!), but it was the best year of Lexi's life!

When Juliette Dubois, the club's adviser and Blakely's drama teacher, suggested they shut down the club for the summer, Lexi was devastated.

"I think it would be wise to take a break, recharge our batteries over the summer," Juliette had said. "You girls are going your separate ways for a few months, and there's no PLC if there's none of you here."

"But *I'm* here!" Lexi piped up. She had no plans to go to camp or on vacation with her family. Both her parents had to work.

"You can't run the entire business by yourself," Kylie said. "Even Mr. Ludwig said he goes to Paris in July and closes down the Golden Spoon. We'll start up again at the end of August, just in time for the back-to-school rush!"

Sadie and Jenna thought this was a good idea. But Lexi was silent. She couldn't imagine a week without baking cupcakes—and without her friends.

"You okay, Lex?" Kylie read her mind.

"I guess. Just sad that PLC is over."

"It's not over!" Jenna insisted. "We'll be back, bigger and better than ever! I'm going to get my *abuela* to give me all her recipes. You know she makes a *cuatro leches* cake instead of *tres leches*? Can you just imagine a four-milk cupcake? Yum!"

"And we'll write to each other all summer," offered Sadie. "Every week! It'll be like we're all still together."

Lexi shrugged. So that was it: PLC would be on break till September. Sadie was off to a basketball camp in North Carolina, Jenna was visiting her grandparents in Ecuador, and Kylie was going to sleepaway camp for the first time in Massachusetts. That left Lexi all alone in New Fairfield, Connecticut.

☆ ☮ ☆

"You could go to Camp Echo Pond with your sister, Ava," Lexi's dad pointed out one night at the dinner table. "You'd have a great time."

Lexi shook her head. "I hate bugs and I can barely doggie paddle."

She remembered last summer, when her parents had enrolled her in Hallard Day Camp—and she came in absolute last place in the swimming relay. Everyone was already out of the pool, drying off, and she still had one lap to go.

"Come on, slow poke!" her counselor Gabby teased. "Stroke! Stroke! Kick! Kick! Big arms!"

Lexi tried her best, but the water stung her eyes and shot up her nose and she was sure she swallowed half the pool.

Everyone in her group had gone back to their bunk when Gabby finally fished her out of the water and handed her a towel. Lexi felt like a prune. Even worse, a pathetic loser prune.

"Nice try," her counselor said. "You gave it your best shot."

But Lexi was completely humiliated. Even the pre-school group could swim faster than she could. No matter how hard she kicked and paddled her arms, she seemed to get nowhere. She sunk like a rock to the bottom of the pool. Once the swim teacher made her go into the deep end to try to tread water. As the rest of her group watched and whispered (she was sure about her!), Lexi clung to the edge of the pool, terrified to let go.

The lifeguard jumped off his tower and kneeled over her. "You okay down there?" he asked, ready to dive in and rescue her.

"Um, yes," she replied, mortified. "Just hangin' out."

"You want a kickboard?"

Lexi glanced at the shallow end where all the little kids in swim diapers were using kickboards.

"No thanks…" she began. But it was too late. The lifeguard handed her a bright pink Dora the Explorer kickboard. "Just hang on and make your way back to four feet."

After that near-drowning Dora disaster, there was no way, no how, she was going to go to Camp Echo Pond!

"Well, they'd teach you to be a good swimmer," Ava assured her. "There's a zip line and canoeing—and Color War is awesome." Lexi remembered the photos Ava had showed her from last summer, her face striped with green war paint. She looked ridiculous.

"I think I'll just stay here and paint pictures—not my face," Lexi said quietly.

Then her mom found out that the Metropolitan Museum of Art in New York City was offering an art intensive program for kids ten and up. This was the first year Lexi was old enough to go. It did sound pretty cool, studying with museum curators and learning the techniques of famous artists for a month in the Big Apple.

"Lexi could stay with my sister, Deanna—she lives a few blocks from the Met," her mom suggested. Dad groaned. Aunt Dee was what he called "a wild card." She was nearly thirty years old and still taking college classes. Last year, she was going to be an accountant (not a good idea, since she was always asking her mom to lend her money!). But this year, she had decided Japanese would be a "way cooler" major—and she might even get to travel.

"She's probably waitressing at night, so that won't work," her dad protested. He was a lawyer and had wanted to be one since he was six, just like his dad and grandpa before him. He couldn't understand anyone who "lacked focus and direction."

"Nope. I checked. Deanna's taking the summer off to

work on her thesis," replied her mom. "So it's perfect. She can watch over Lexi for the four weeks."

Her dad finally gave in, although he suspected that Lexi would be watching over Aunt Dee and not vice versa. Her mom's kid sister was colorful and spontaneous—everything Lexi secretly wished she could be. She wore funny, floppy hats and owned a pair of clogs in every color of the rainbow. She ate cold pizza for breakfast and packed pickle chips in her purse. She was never embarrassed, never sorry, and never too shy to speak her mind.

When Lexi stepped off the train at Grand Central Terminal with her mom, Aunt Dee was waiting on the track, holding a big sign that read "Welcome to NYC!" She was jumping up and down, whistling through her teeth, making sure they spotted her in the lunch hour crowds pouring out of the train and into the station. Lexi giggled—Dee was hard to miss!

"How's my brilliantabulous niece Alexandra?" Dee asked, hugging her.

"Good!" Lexi replied. And for the first time in a few weeks, she actually felt good. She was excited to be in the Big Apple, and Dee had plans…lots of plans.

"So first, I thought we'd grab some pizza at Two Boots and cheesecake at Junior's," she began. "You hungry?"

Lexi nodded and her stomach rumbled to second the motion.

"Just make sure you listen to your aunt…and don't talk to strangers…or wander off…" her mom reminded her. "And don't forget to use hand sanitizer!" She'd packed Lexi's bag with at least six bottles of it!

"Your mom is a worrywart," Dee shot back. "We'll be just fine. Right, Lexi?"

Lexi nodded. If Grand Central was any indication, New York City was a pretty wild, crazy, crowded place. But her aunt seemed to love it—and she fit in perfectly. Lexi kissed her mom good-bye and Dee pulled her along.

"I thought we'd take a walk through Times Square, maybe check out the huge Ferris wheel in Toys'R'Us, Ripley's Believe It or Not! Museum…" her aunt suggested.

Lexi could barely catch her breath as they zigzagged through all the commuters. Grand Central was bigger and more bustling than she had remembered it. She hadn't been here since first grade, when her class took a trip to see the toy train exhibit at Christmastime.

"Look up!" Aunt Dee said, pointing to the turquoise

ceiling covered in constellations. "It's the only place in New York City where you can see the stars during the day…unless you count a Broadway matinee. But that's not till next Wednesday!"

Lexi noticed that everyone seemed to be in an awfully big hurry. There was a huge four-sided clock in the center of the information booth. Everyone was checking the time, rushing to make their trains. One lady in a pinstripe suit was talking on her cellphone and almost ran Lexi over.

"Watch where you're going!" she snapped at Lexi.

Aunt Dee stuck out her tongue at the woman and barreled straight ahead, down the escalator, and through the dining concourse. Lexi noticed there were lots of different foods on display: sushi, salads, hot and crusty loaves of bread, rich chocolate candies. Then her eye caught a small bakery stand in the corner filled with pastries…and cupcakes!

"Can we stop here, please, Aunt Dee?" she pleaded. She simply had to check out the competition.

"Sure! Dessert before lunch. My kind of gal!" Dee replied.

Lexi surveyed the trays of frosted cupcakes. They were nothing fancy: just simple vanilla and chocolate icing with rainbow sprinkles on top. "I'll take a chocolate," she said, handing the saleswoman two dollars. She took a bite and wrinkled her nose.

"Oh, Jenna would just hate this. It tastes like it's been sitting in a fridge for days!" she exclaimed.

Aunt Dee broke off a corner of the cake. "Tastes okay to me."

"No, Kylie is really particular about the frosting to cupcake ratio. This is way too much frosting. It overpowers all the other flavors."

"You sound like you know what you're talking about," the saleswoman said. "Are you a professional baker?"

Lexi smiled. "Yes! My friends and I have this amazing cupcake club called Peace, Love, and Cupcakes!" Then she caught herself. "I mean, we *had* this amazing club. It's kind of on hold at the moment."

"Oh, that's really too bad," the woman replied. She handed Lexi a vanilla cupcake. "Maybe you'd like this one better?"

"Thanks," she answered. And yes, it was fresher tasting and even had a pink rose piped on top in buttercream. But it didn't make her miss her friends and PLC any less.

Over a pepperoni pizza for lunch, Lexi was a bit distracted, even when Aunt Dee took out a map and unfolded it practically in her plate. She couldn't help thinking about Kylie, Sadie, and Jenna. What were they doing right now? Were they thinking about her too? She doubted it!

"You see this?" Dee asked, circling a street on the map with a neon pink highlighter pen she just happened to carry in her purse. "This is where I live. Right near Central Park, right near the Met."

Lexi flicked some basil leaves off her slice.

"Do you snore?" Dee suddenly asked.

"Huh?" Lexi snapped to attention.

"Do you snore? It's a simple question." She twirled a goocy strand of mozzarella cheese around her finger.

"I don't think so," Lexi answered. What if her aunt didn't really *want* her staying with her for the next few weeks? She had never thought of that…

"Well, we'll have to do something about that," Dee said, slamming her hand on the table. "I insist that all my roommates snore, leave dirty laundry on the floor, and watch late night TV. Extra points if you clog the toilet and it overflows."

Lexi laughed so hard, Sprite sprayed out of her nose.

"Well, that's better!" Dee said, patting her on the back. "No Lexi long faces in my apartment." She winked and held up her Diet Coke can to offer a toast.

"To an August of fun!"

Lexi clinked her can. "To fun!"

Bright Lights, Big City

In just her first weekend in Manhattan, Lexi learned so much about the Big Apple! Aunt Dee was an encyclopedia of crazy facts and figures. She took her to the Top of the Rock, seventy floors straight up, and asked if she knew how many feet high they were in the air.

"Go on…take a guess," Dee teased, popping a quarter in a telescope so they could zoom in on the city skyline.

"Um, five hundred?" Lexi ventured.

"Nope! Higher!"

"Six hundred?"

"Keep goin'!"

"Seven hundred?" Lexi was determined to get the number.

"Give up?" Dee taunted her. "You were so close! Eight hundred and fifty feet. And that," she said, pointing, "is the Chrysler Building, the Empire State Building, and the Brooklyn Bridge."

Lexi couldn't believe how huge the city was from this view. It seemed to go on forever and ever.

"We're going to see it all," Dee promised her.

Lexi gasped. All this? "Not in one day, please, Aunt Dee! My feet are killing me!"

The telescope clicked off. "Nope. I need at least two days for that," Dee teased.

They took the elevator back down and Lexi's ears popped. Once on the street, Dee hailed a cab and they piled in. "Eighty-Second and Fifth," she instructed the driver. "Do you know why taxis in New York are yellow?" she asked Lexi.

Lexi pondered for a moment. "Because yellow is a happy color and it makes people happy when they can stop walking and rest their tired toes?"

"Close. It's yellow because that's the easiest color to spot. At least that's what John Hertz, the company's founder thought."

The cab dropped them in front of the steps of the Met, and Lexi gazed up at them in amazement. There were people sitting and having a snack, others chattering away in all different languages.

Dee bought them dinner from a hot dog cart parked in front.

"Did you know that Babe Ruth once ate twelve hot dogs between a double header baseball game?" she said, piling relish, mustard, ketchup, and mayo on her dog.

When the vendor offered Lexi some sauerkraut, ketchup, mustard, or chopped onions, she covered her plate. "No thanks. I like mine plain."

Dee raised an eyebrow. "What's your record, Lex? Could you break Babe Ruth's dozen down the hatch?"

Lexi shrugged. "I don't think I could eat more than two. Maybe three if I was starving." But she had to admit, NYC hot dogs from street carts did taste so much more delicious than the ones her dad made on the grill back home. There was something about New York that just made everything so much *better*.

Lexi loved how the streets seemed to have their own pulse, "the heartbeat of the city" Dee called it. At first, she couldn't feel it (and frankly thought her aunt was a little wacky). But after walking around, all over Midtown, downtown, and the Upper East Side, she understood what Dee was talking about. New York had a vibration. She could feel it running just beneath the concrete. It wasn't the rumble of the subways. It wasn't even the hundreds of pairs of feet pounding the pavement. It was an energy.

Lexi felt it sweeping her along, as if she was caught in some current, racing upstream. It was exciting and a little scary all at once.

"Toto, we're not in Kansas anymore," Dee declared, taking a bite of her hot dog with all the fixings and sitting down on the Met's steps.

"What does that mean?" Lexi asked, settling beside her.

"It means NYC is far from New Fairfield," she explained.

"It was only a few stops on the train," Lexi corrected her. "Maybe just fifty miles."

"I don't mean that," Dee insisted. "I mean you have to think and act like a New Yorker. Take some chances!"

She squirted a glob of hot sauce out of a packet and onto Lexi's hot dog. Lexi gulped; she was afraid it would be super spicy and set her mouth on fire. But she was so hungry, and it smelled so good.

"Nothing ventured, nothing gained," Dee said, licking her lips.

Lexi closed her eyes and took a small nibble. It was hot all right—it made her tongue tingle. But it was delicious!

"I like it!" Lexi announced. "I guess, like a cupcake, a hot dog needs a topping."

☆ ☮ ☆

That wasn't the only culinary adventure Aunt Dee took her on. On a Wednesday, they ventured down to Hell's Kitchen, and her aunt's favorite little French bistro for a pre-theater meal. It had a garden out back and served all kinds of French delicacies—like smelly truffles, snails, and frog legs!

"Oh, I couldn't," Lexi insisted when her aunt put a garlicky snail on a small fork and handed it to her.

"Ya don't know what you're missing!" Dee said, popping it in her mouth. "Escargot is *magnifique!*"

So Lexi closed her eyes and took a taste. The escargot was kind of slimy on her tongue, but it had a nice, buttery flavor.

"Not bad, right?" Dee asked. "Maybe you could make an escargot cupcake one day!"

Lexi grimaced at the thought. "Not even for April Fool's Day. That would be just too gross!" she giggled.

They went to see a Broadway musical with lots of chorus girls kicking up their heels and a leading man who danced around in tap shoes and a bow tie. He and the leading lady crooned silly love songs to each other, stuff like, "I've got a crush on you, sweetie pie!" and "Embrace me, my sweet embraceable you!" At the end of the show, there was a big, over-the-top white wedding, with swans, silver sequins, and giant wedding bells.

"Mush," Aunt Dee declared. "But good mush." They left the theater, humming a Gershwin tune.

"Are you going to get married soon, Aunt Dee?" Lexi asked suddenly.

"Whoa! I don't even have a boyfriend. Slow down!" her aunt chuckled.

Lexi wondered what had happened to her last serious boyfriend, E.J. He was a film student at NYU, and Dee had brought him to Thanksgiving dinner in Connecticut. He had cool, spiky hair and wore sunglasses at night. Lexi liked him a lot, but her parents frowned when he put his feet up on their coffee table.

"E.J. and I broke up. He wanted to go to Hollywood. I wanted to stay here. I love New York too much to leave it. So *hasta la vista*, baby!"

Her aunt was trying to joke about it, but Lexi could sense she was sadder than she let on. Though she tried to come off like a tough cookie, Dee loved sappy, romantic musicals. She believed in true love.

"How about you? You have a boyfriend?" Dee tried to change the subject.

"Me? I'm only ten!" Lexi protested.

"I had a boyfriend when I was ten. Just ask your mother. His name was Nathaniel Rothstein. He played the drums. He was dreamy."

Lexi giggled. "Nathaniel? What kind of a name is Nathaniel?"

"I agree, the name was a little lame. But Nate was a really nice boy, the first boy to ever notice me. He shared his chocolate milk with me in the cafeteria. Two straws. We were inseparable all through fourth and fifth grade before he moved to Arizona."

Lexi tried to picture her aunt and Nathaniel at age ten, slurping chocolate milk and singing, "S'wonderful… s'marvelous…that you should care for me!" to each other, just like they'd seen in the show. She wondered if Dee wore floppy hats back then…

"You'll have a boyfriend soon, Lexi," Aunt Dee assured her.

Lexi shook her head. "I don't think so. I'm just too shy. I'd panic if a boy talked to me."

"Well then, we have our work cut out for us these next few weeks," Dee said, linking arms with her. "There's some lucky guy out there just waiting to sweep you off your feet!" She twirled Lexi around, right in the middle of Broadway.

Lexi was too busy with her art classes at the Met to even think about falling in love. She was too in love with the museum! Every day, she walked through the Great Hall, gazing up at the soaring arches, and made her away through the exhibits, trying to take it all in. There were so many beautiful paintings and sculptures. She loved Cézanne's still lifes the most, how he made even common objects like a ginger jar, a teacup, or a pile of apples take on a magical glow on the canvas. Like in a 3-D movie, the objects seem to leap out at her.

"What are you painting, Lexi?" her instructor Mr. Ruffalo asked, peering over her shoulder. Lexi gulped. She hated to be put on the spot. Her heart raced and she could feel her cheeks burn as her fellow art students gathered around. Plus Mr. Ruffalo was a little scary. He wore these big, round black glasses that made him look like a wise old owl. She was sure he could see right through a painting—and right through a person. So she was very, very careful when she answered.

"Um, just a still life of some cupcakes," Lexi replied.

Mr. Ruffalo pursed his lips. "Hmmm…very interesting. Your use of blue light in the background to illuminate the red frosting of the cupcakes. The bottle of vanilla next to them. It's very Cézanne."

Oh my gosh! Did he just compare me to a famous French impressionist? Lexi couldn't wait till her aunt met her at the front steps of the museum that afternoon to tell her.

"Aunt Dee! Aunt Dee!" she squealed. "You have to come see this!" She dragged her into a small gallery on the second floor of the museum.

"Look at this!" she said, flipping through her portfolio and pulling out her still life painting.

"It's very nice, Lex…"

"And this," she said, spinning Dee around to face a wall of the gallery. "Look at this!"

Dee pondered the painting hanging in front of them. It was a pile of apples with a brown bottle next to them.

"Uh-huh," she said simply. "Nice apples?"

"It's Cézanne! Mr. Ruffalo said I did a great job capturing the technique of Cézanne!"

Aunt Dee stared harder at the painting on the wall. "Okay, but it just doesn't float my boat," she replied. "Not enough colors. It's kind of boring."

21

There was an audible gasp behind them. Lexi noticed a few Japanese tourists staring. She prayed that Dee wouldn't offer her opinion in their native language.

"Well, it's supposed to be like that. Cézanne took months to finish this piece."

"Well, that explains it. He spent too much time cooped up inside!"

Lexi huffed and put her painting back in her portfolio. It was no use—Aunt Dee was simply not a fan of Impressionist art.

Dee yawned. "Come on. Let's get outta here and have some *real* fun!"

They spent the rest of the afternoon in Central Park, riding the carousel, pitching pennies into the Bethesda Fountain, and taking a rowboat out on the lake.

Lexi was a little nervous she'd tip over and fall in the water, especially when Dee rocked the boat as she rowed. "I'm not a really good swimmer," she confided in her aunt, holding on to the boat's sides with an iron grip.

"Me neither," said Dee. "But I'm a good floater!"

Then they sat in the sheep meadow, licking Popsicles they bought from an ice cream cart. The red and yellow pop dripped all over Dee's white tank top, but she didn't seem to care. "Makes a cool tie-dye pattern, don't ya think?" she said, rubbing it in with a napkin.

Lexi laughed. Sometimes Aunt Dee seemed more like a kid than a grown-up, but Lexi loved that about her (even if it drove her father crazy!). She pulled a notebook and markers out of her backpack and started drawing.

"What's that?" Dee asked, watching her.

"It's an idea for a cupcake," Lexi replied. "I call it Friday in the Park with Dee." On the red and yellow tie-dye frosting, she drew a boat, a carousel horse, and a Popsicle. "I could sculpt these out of fondant."

"Edible art. I like it," Dee said, rolling over in the grass to tan her back. "It's a lot better than that Cézanne dude we saw in the museum!"

☆ ☮ ☆

By the middle of August, Lexi had filled an entire notebook with cupcake ideas and drawings. No matter what painting or sculpture she studied at the Met, she could also envision it as a delicious cupcake.

"I was thinking I could do tiny dots in different colors of frosting to look like a Seurat painting," she explained.

Aunt Dee looked puzzled. "A *sir what?*"

"*Sir-rah*," Lexi giggled. "Georges Seurat. He was a French postimpressionist. And when you look at his paintings up close, all you see is lots of little dots. But when you step back, you see the big picture."

"Hmm. Sounds complicated. But if anyone can do it, kiddo, you can!"

With Aunt Dee's vote of confidence, Lexi drew Back-to-School cupcakes topped with tiny fondant rulers and pencils, and cupcakes sprinkled with red sugar crystals to look like shiny apples. Then there was her favorite design: a fudge brownie cupcake for Valentine's Day with a marshmallow heart on top. She called it Bake Me, I'm Yours. Aunt Dee had suggested the heart. She sprinkled mini marshmallows on practically everything—even brussels sprouts. "Marshmallows make the world a better place," she declared.

Thanks to her aunt, Lexi got to see parts of NYC she didn't even know existed: the Lower East Side (Aunt Dee's fave place to buy pickle chips), the South Street Seaport, Randall's Island. They rode the rickety Cyclone roller coaster at Coney Island and sipped Earl Grey tea at Tea & Sympathy in the Village. Aunt Dee knew all the best places and filled every day with surprises.

"What about clotted cream frosting?" her aunt asked, smearing cream and jelly on a warm-from-the-oven cinnamon scone. "You could make a recipe for it on a vanilla cupcake."

"That could be delicious," Lexi said, noting it in her notebook. "And I could do an Earl Gray tea-infused frosting too. It would go great on a dark chocolate cupcake."

"Mmmm." Dee nodded. "Don't forget to add the marshmallows on top."

☆ ☮ ☆

Lexi couldn't wait to share her cupcake ideas with her friends! In all the activity of the past four weeks, she'd almost forgotten how much she'd missed them. Now she'd miss Aunt Dee.

"You'll call me with weekly updates, right?" Dee asked, hugging her on the Metro North platform.

"I will!" Lexi said. "Thank you for the most amazing summer I've ever had."

"And you won't forget everything I taught you: hot sauce on hot dogs and escargot cupcakes."

Lexi laughed. "You taught me a lot more than that!"

Her aunt handed her a little package, bundled in comic

book pages. Even the wrapping made Lexi smile. "For you! A souvenir," Dee said.

Lexi tore it open. Inside was a T-shirt with I ♥ NY on it.

"I love it!" Lexi said. "I'll wear it my first day of fifth grade." She climbed on the train and waved good-bye as it pulled out of the station, chugging her back home to New Fairfield.

☆ ☮ ☆

When she got to her stop, her parents and her big sister, Ava, were all waiting for her. Lexi breathed a sigh of relief. Though she loved the city, it was "s'wonderful" to be back where she belonged. Plus, it was her first time riding a train alone! Amazingly, she hadn't been scared. She felt like a real New Yorker who could handle just about anything!

"Thought we'd have a picnic tonight by Candlewood Lake," her dad suggested.

"I'd rather just hang out at home," Lexi replied. What she really wanted to do was check her email and see if any of her PLC mates had come home yet.

Her room seemed smaller somehow—maybe she'd grown? Or maybe everything in New Fairfield looked tiny when compared to the huge city?

"I swear, I didn't touch any of your stuff," her sister, Ava, said, flopping down on her bed. "How was Aunt Dee? How was New York?"

"Great!" Lexi replied. "I learned so much. How was camp?"

Ava launched into a whole, long-winded account of how she'd starred in the camp musical (she'd played Glinda in *Wicked*) and scored the winning soccer goal for her bunk. Was there anything Ava couldn't do expertly, Lexi wondered. It all came so easily to her.

Plus, there was a boy! A seventh grader in the neighboring boys camp named Grayson. "He gave me his email and we're going to FaceTime on our iPads," Ava rambled on. "He told me I was pretty!"

Ava *was* pretty. And smart. And confident. Ugh.

"Well, I guess you wanna be alone to unpack," Ava said. "Glad to have you home, sis!" She shut Lexi's bedroom door and left her alone. Lexi's dog, Poochie, hopped up on her bed and planted a wet, welcome-home kiss on her nose. She was scratching his tummy when she noticed something on her desk: letters! Her friends had finally answered! Lexi's face lit up and she tore into them.

"They made me point guard this week!" Sadie wrote. "I'm learning so much about basketball. This is the best place ever!"

"My *abuela* is teaching me to knit," wrote Jenna. "You should see the cool scarf I'm making!"

Jenna and Sadie sounded so busy—and so happy to be away. Their letters were way too short. But it was Kylie's postcard that was the most upsetting: "Camp rocks! I wish I never had to leave Camp Chicopee!"

Lexi gulped. What if Kylie forgot all about their cupcake club? What if she didn't want to do it again in fifth grade? What if all her friends abandoned her come September? What if PLC was history?

The ding of her computer shook her out of this horrible thought and brought her back to reality. She checked the message and her spirits soared when she saw the address: CupcakeKylie@carson.net. She clicked to open it:

Hey, PLC-ers! Guess who just got home from camp? R U ready to bake some cupcakes? XO, Kylie

Lexi emailed back from artsygirl10@poole.net:

Welcome home! I missed u! Can't wait! XO, Lexi

She beamed when she hit the Send button. Everything was

fine. Their Cupcake Club was fine. Nothing had changed over the summer. And in no time, Peace, Love, and Cupcakes would be sweetly in swing again!

3

Frenemies?

"Kylie!" Lexi exclaimed as her friend opened the front door to her house. She hugged her so tightly, Kylie could barely breathe.

"Lexi! I'm so glad to see you too! But I'm not a pastry bag—don't squeeze so hard," she laughed.

"I'm sorry," Lexi apologized. "I'm just so happy to see you."

Kylie looked different: she was tan, and her hair, once a deep, dark brown, now shimmered with honey-colored highlights from being in the sun. Her nose and cheeks were speckled with freckles, and she wore tiny gold studs in her ears.

"You got your ears pierced!" Lexi exclaimed. "Awesome!"

"My mom promised I could for the beginning of fifth grade," Kylie said. "I want cupcake earrings for Hanukkah this year. Maybe little dangly red velvets?"

"You look so cool!" Lexi said. She threw her arms around her friend again. "I just missed you so much! It feels like summer vacation went on forever and ever."

"Really? I thought it flew by," Kylie said. "One day I was checking into my bunk at Camp Chicopee, and the next day the bus was driving me back home. I passed my deepwater test, rode horses, and roasted marshmallows over a campfire! And I made so many new friends!"

"You did?" Lexi asked. It felt strange to think of her BFF sharing secrets with anyone but her, Jenna, and Sadie.

"Tons! And guess what? One of them, Delaney, is crazy about vampires, just like I am! We talked about *Twilight* and *Dracula* for hours and scared everyone around the campfire with bloody, creepy stories."

"Wow. That's great," Lexi said. She felt a pang of jealousy. She didn't want Kylie to have tons of other friends. Where would that leave her?

"And Delaney even lives in Danbury, which is really close by. I told her maybe she could stop in on the weekends and help us bake cupcakes."

Lexi's eyes grew wide. "You told her she could join PLC?"

"Well, not exactly," continued Kylie. "But that's not a bad idea. We could probably use another pair of hands, especially when the orders start rolling in again. And Delaney is amazingly cool. She knows *every* Lady Gaga song by heart!"

Lexi bit her lip. She wanted to scream at Kylie, "I don't care if she's cool! I don't care if you liked her in camp! I don't care if she can sing 'Born This Way' *backward*! PLC is *our* club!" But instead, she shrugged and headed for the kitchen.

Jenna was already nibbling chocolate chips out of the bag.

"*Amiga!*" she squealed, picking up Lexi and swinging her around.

Lexi smiled, but she was still upset from her talk with Kylie. She tried to shake it off and be bright and cheery. "Jenna, you look great! You cut your hair!" Jenna's waist-long braid was now replaced with bouncy, shoulder-length waves. Her hair was dark and shiny and reminded Lexi of a rich chocolate ganache.

"You like it? My cousins thought it made me look more 'sophisticated.' More like a fifth grader. And check out this awesome scarf I knitted!" She rested a hand on her hip and struck a pose.

"I think you look awesome, Jenna," said Kylie, grabbing her purple apron and tying it around her waist. "Did you have fun in Ecuador with your family?"

"It was *fantástico!*" Jenna enthused. "My *abuela* is the most amazing cook, and she taught me all her secrets. I can make the best *arroz con pollo* now. And I got to swim in the sea with dolphins and turtles and bike around a volcano!"

"Wow! A volcano?" Kylie gasped. "With lava and smoke and everything? That tops my zip-lining for sure."

Zip-lining? Swimming with dolphins? Volcanoes? Lexi's summer in the city couldn't compare to her friends' adventures. And even worse, Kylie and Jenna looked and seemed so much more grown-up.

"We're just waiting for Sadie, and we can get down to business," Kylie said. "I think we should start putting up some Back-to-School Cupcake flyers and emailing our clients…"

"I thought the same thing!" said Lexi, opening to a page in her sketchbook. She had drawn a cupcake with a book and ruler on top. Across the page she wrote "A is for Awesome! B is for Best! C is for Cupcakes! Happy Back to School from Peace, Love, and Cupcakes!"

"Wow, you come prepared!" said Jenna. "That's really clever."

Kylie nodded. "I love it. Just one thing I would change: the frosting should probably be another color, not yellow."

Lexi winced. "Well, yellow is the color of a school bus. That's why I chose it," she said quietly.

"I get it," said Kylie. "But yellow makes me think of

sour lemons. And people want to start the school year off sweet, not sour, right?"

Lexi stared down at her sneakers. "Um, I guess so. But I really think the yellow pops..."

"Maybe bright pink or purple?" Kylie continued.

"How about tie-dye—always a crowd-pleaser?" suggested Jenna.

Lexi wished she could really say what she was thinking. Her Aunt Dee would. She would never let anyone drown out her opinions. She would simply stand up, shoulders back, head held high, and announce what she thought. But if I do that, thought Lexi, my friends might be angry with me. Then again, I'm an important member of this club. They can't do beautiful, artistic cupcakes without me!

Lexi took a deep breath and declared loudly, "The cupcakes should be yellow!"

Kylie and Jenna looked stunned. They had never seen Lexi take a stand so strongly. In fact, they'd never heard her raise her voice at all!

"Yellow? Really?" said Kylie. "I don't know..."

"I *do* know," replied Lexi. "I've spent the whole summer studying art, and yellow is a bright, happy color. It's the color of Van Gogh's *Sunflowers.*"

"But I really think white would be better—a delicious vanilla bean frosting," Kylie persisted.

Lexi stood her ground: "Yellow!"

"Hey, cupcakers!" called Sadie, knocking on the front door. "Anybody home?"

"In here!" shouted Jenna. She was relieved that Sadie had arrived to help referee. Sadie hugged and high-fived all the girls.

"Oh my gosh, did you get taller? How could you possibly get any taller?" Jenna teased her friend. "You're going to be ten feet tall by middle school!" Sadie straddled the kitchen stool with her long legs and took off her baseball cap.

"And you cut your hair while mine got longer!" Sadie said. Her once curly short 'do was now a shoulder-length ponytail. "Ya like? My brothers say I look like a girl now. Whatever!"

Kylie gave her the thumbs-up and playfully tugged at her pony. "We need your help with Back-to-School cupcakes, Sadie," she began, holding up Lexi's sketch. "What do you think?"

Sadie tilted her head one way, than the other, looking at the cupcake drawing from every angle. "I think it's cool."

Lexi smirked. "Told you, Kylie."

"But don't you think yellow is the wrong color for the frosting?" Kylie elbowed Sadie.

"Um, I guess?" said Sadie. "Maybe it should be green, like the color of the Blakely basketball uniforms?"

"Ugh!" Lexi cried. "Is everyone going to agree with Kylie? Why does she get to make all the decisions for Peace, Love, and Cupcakes?"

"Well, she *is* the president of our club," Sadie said, trying to help. "Kind of like the captain of the team. The captain always calls the shots."

Lexi could feel her temper bubbling up inside her like the time she was trying to make chocolate ganache and overheated cream on the stove. It suddenly swelled up and exploded over the sides of the pot. Lexi felt the same way. She was going to explode!

"I'm tired of Kylie calling the shots!" she finally yelled. "She's always bossing us around!"

"I'm bossy?" Kylie said. "You're the one who said the cupcakes *have* to be yellow."

Jenna looked puzzled. "What's going on? Why are you guys fighting like this? I thought everyone would be so happy to see each other!"

"I was," said Lexi. "Until Kylie told me she's inviting her *new* friends to join PLC."

"We never talked about letting more people join," said Sadie. "I'm not great with math, but I know that if we divide up our profits more ways, they'll be less for each of us."

"Plus, we built PLC from scratch," Jenna pointed out. "It's our cupcake club—we don't want tons of people getting involved. Too many cooks spoil the cupcake batter."

"I said *one* friend," insisted Kylie. "My camp friend, Delaney. I thought she could help if we get really busy."

Jenna shrugged. "Well, maybe *that* would be okay. Kind of like a baking assistant. Can we make her do the hard stuff, like crack eggs and roll fondant?"

Lexi fumed. "Stop siding with her! We worked so hard last year to make PLC a success, and now we're going to let someone who doesn't know the first thing about cupcakes come in and ruin it?"

Kylie sighed. "Okay, Lexi, if it really means that much to you, I'll tell Delaney she can't help." She tried to put her arm around her friend, but Lexi pulled away.

"Fine," she said, then ran out of the kitchen, practically knocking Mrs. Carson over in the process.

"Wow, where was Lexi going in such a hurry?" Kylie's mom asked.

Kylie shrugged. "She just got mad at everything I said. It was weird."

"Maybe she's nervous about starting fifth grade," her mom suggested. "It's a big year. Let her cool down. I'm sure once you guys get back to baking, everything will smooth out between you."

Lexi bolted out the front door of Kylie's house onto Frisbee Street, hopped on her bicycle, and pedaled straight for her home three blocks away. She was nearly there when she parked her bike, sat down on the curb, and rested her head in her hands. She didn't want her mom to see her like this and ask what was wrong.

Honestly, she didn't know! She had no idea why she was so mad at Kylie or why her talking about other friends or changing the color of frosting made her feel so left out. The tears rolled down her cheeks and landed on the cover of the sketchbook in her lap, turning the markered letters *PLC* into a rainbow-colored puddle.

The entire day had been nothing like how she'd imagined

it. Instead of the girls giggling in the kitchen and trying out yummy new cupcake recipes, there was just arguing and hurt feelings. What was wrong with Kylie? Why was she trying to ruin PLC? And why didn't Jenna or Sadie speak up and stop her? The fun they had last year felt a million miles away. Why was everything changing?

"Lexi?" said a voice suddenly.

It was Kylie. She had followed her. "Can I talk to you?"

Lexi wiped the tears away with the back of her hoodie sleeve. "What do you want?"

"I'm sorry. *Really* sorry. I didn't mean to make you cry."

"Whatever." Lexi sniffed. She was trying her hardest to sound tough.

"I was just so excited to tell you all about camp. I didn't know it would make you feel bad. I didn't even get to ask you how your summer was."

Lexi shrugged. "Fine."

"Please come back to my house. We want to bake a batch of Back-to-School cupcakes—and we can't do it without you."

"You can't?" Lexi dried her tears.

"Have you seen the way Jenna pipes? She'll use up the entire bag of frosting on one cupcake!"

Lexi managed a weak smile. "She does like a mountain of frosting, doesn't she?"

"*Yellow* frosting. We decided it would catch people's eyes and look great in the Golden Spoon's window. You were right," replied Kylie. "Please come back."

Lexi nodded and stood up. "Thanks, Kylie."

Kylie smiled and linked arms with Lexi for the walk. "What are friends for?"

Back to School

The first day of fifth grade at Blakely Elementary started off with a bang.

"You won't believe it," Lexi said, catching up with Kylie, Sadie, and Jenna at lunch. "Jeremy Saperstone accidentally blew up our science experiment!"

"What? How?" the girls gasped.

"It was so crazy! We were supposed to combine a little vinegar and baking soda so it would fizz. But Jeremy poured in too much and put a lid on the container so Mr. Reidy wouldn't see. Then he shook it up and the lid blew off, and the whole table was covered with a foamy mess!"

"Did he get in trouble?" asked Jenna.

"No. He explained that he was trying to prove the powerful chemical reaction between acetic acid and sodium bicarbonate, and Mr. Reidy was very impressed. Jeremy's really smart!" Lexi unpacked her lunch. "I'm lucky to have him as my science partner."

Jenna raised an eyebrow. "Hmmm…is it me, or does somebody sound like she has a crush on Jeremy Saperstone?"

Sadie and Kylie giggled. "No! I mean, that's ridiculous!" said Lexi, taking a big bite out of her cream cheese and cucumber sandwich. "I just said he's smart, that's all."

"And cute. Kind of like Justin Bieber, don't you think?" Kylie teased.

"No, I don't think he's cute," Lexi insisted. "And I'm not talking about this anymore."

"If you say so," said Jenna, winking at Lexi. "But we can keep a secret."

"Ugh," groaned Lexi, ducking her head under the lid of her lunch box. "I'm sorry I mentioned it!"

☆ ☮ ☆

Right after school, Peace, Love, and Cupcakes had its first official meeting with Juliette. "Welcome back, girls!" she said, hugging each of them. "You all got so tall—and, Jenna, I love your new 'do! And, Kylie, you got your ears pierced! Fill me in, girls! What's new with all of you?"

"Why don't you tell her about your crush on Jeremy?" Jenna teased Lexi.

Lexi's cheeks turned red. "Seriously? Can you please stop? I am *not* crushing on him." Lexi retreated into a corner. Juliette followed.

"'The lady doth protest too much,'" her teacher said quietly.

"What does that mean?" asked Lexi.

"It's a line from Shakespeare's *Hamlet*. It means if there wasn't some truth to it, you wouldn't get so upset with what your friends are teasing you about."

Lexi thought for a minute. "So what? I mean, what if I do think Jeremy is a little cute? And smart. Is that such a big deal?"

"No, it's not. And it's your business, no one else's. Just ignore them, Lexi. The more you get mad—"

"The more they'll tease me, I get it."

Juliette smiled. "Good! Let's get down to baking business!"

The girls ran through their entire list of special orders for the next few weeks, everything from a *Star Wars*–themed birthday party (Jenna suggested Darth Vader Dark Chocolate Cupcakes) to a luncheon for the Horticulture Society (Lexi was excited to pipe cupcakes that looked like chrysanthemums).

"Principal Fontina asked if we could make 750 cupcakes to sell at the Back-to-School Bash in two weeks," said Juliette. "Doable?"

"I dunno," said Sadie, eyeing her schedule. "I have track team tryouts next Thursday and basketball practice Fridays, plus special tutoring every Monday for my dyslexia. You should see the pile of homework I have—and it's just the first day!"

"I can make the fondant decorations ahead of time, so we'll just have to bake and pipe," said Lexi. "That should cut down a lot on the time we need to make them. How about this?"

She pulled out her summer sketchbook and showed the girls her drawing of a cupcake topped with a red fondant apple. "It's very simple to make—a little ball with a stem, and I can shine it up with edible glitter."

"Cute!" said Jenna. "We could call them 'Appealing Cupcakes.' Get it? Apples have a peel?"

"I was thinking an apple cinnamon cupcake with a salted caramel butter cream," continued Lexi.

"Yum!" said Sadie. "Great idea, Lex! How did you come up with it?"

"My Aunt Dee. She dips pretzels in caramel and it's really good."

Kylie nodded. "I like it. And we could bake an extra 250 for Mr. Ludwig at the Golden Spoon as the week's special."

"I think Principal Fontina will be very happy," said Juliette. "What other events do we have coming up?"

Kylie's hand shot up. "Only my favorite holiday, Halloween! I am counting the days! What should we make this year? Ghostly Guava? Mummy Marshmallow? Bloody Red Velvet?"

Once again, Lexi flipped through the pages of her sketchbook. "How about this?" she said, holding up a drawing of an oozing eyeball on top of a cupcake. "I call it, 'Eye Love Halloween!'" She giggled at her own pun.

"It's gross—which is a good thing for Halloween," said Jenna.

"But we could go even grosser! How about a bloody knife sticking out of a cupcake?" said Sadie.

"How about we pipe pink frosting on a cupcake and make it look like brains?" said Kylie with a devilish glint in her eye. She pulled her notebook out and produced a sketch.

"Ewww!" squealed Jenna and Sadie. "That's awesome!"

Lexi was quiet. "What do you think, Lexi?" asked Juliette.

Lexi closed her sketchbook. "I think nobody cares what I think," she said.

"That isn't true, Lex!" said Kylie. "We make decisions as a club. Every idea is important!"

"Sure, as long as they're *your* ideas," Lexi replied.

"Here we go again," sighed Jenna. "It's going to be another fight."

Juliette clapped her hands together to get everyone's attention. "Will someone please tell me what's going here? What happened to the *peace* in Peace, Love, and Cupcakes?"

Neither Kylie or Lexi responded. "Okay then," said Juliette. "I'm all for drama, but when it comes to theater, not cupcakes. What can we do to compromise?"

Lexi grabbed her pink-colored pencil and sketched a cupcake with fat, pink, zigzag lines—it looked just like brains. She held it up to Kylie. "I could use a number ten round tip to pipe the frosting."

Kylie smiled. "Love it. That's so much better than my flat pink frosting."

"Now that's using your brains, Lex," joked Jenna. The girls all groaned at the joke.

"I suggest we do both eyeballs *and* brains for Halloween," added Juliette. "Since they're both inspired ideas." Lexi and Kylie nodded. It sounded fair.

Sadie glanced at the clock on the wall. "Uh-oh. It's 3:25—my mom's picking me up in five minutes!"

"Then this meeting of PLC is adjourned," said Kylie,

gathering up her notebook. She looked over at Lexi, real-
izing that she might have sounded too bossy. "Unless we
have something more to talk about?"

Lexi shook her head. She was done talking. It only
seemed to get her into more trouble, whether it was about
her cupcake ideas or her secret crush on Jeremy.

"'Parting is such sweet sorrow,'" sighed Juliette.

Lexi looked confused. "What does that mean?" Her
teacher was certainly speaking in strange riddles today.

"It's from *Romeo and Juliet*," Juliette replied. "It means
saying good-bye is both sad and happy. I guess I have
Shakespeare on the brain."

"Why?" asked Lexi.

Juliette smiled mischievously. "That's for me to know
and you guys to find out…tomorrow in drama class."

When Lexi walked into third-period drama class Tuesday morning, she could barely believe her eyes. There was Juliette wearing a long, flowing, purple velvet gown and a strange crocheted cap on her head.

"Um, does she think it's Halloween? 'Cause that's not for at least a month and a half," Meredith Mitchell whispered to Emily Dutter.

Lexi had to agree, Juliette looked very strange. Why would her teacher show up to school in such a crazy costume? She looked like she had stepped out of another time...or a Disney princess movie!

Lexi saw that Kylie was waving, motioning for her to come sit with her. But just then, she spied Jeremy in the back row of the classroom. He was wearing a Yankees shirt, and his bangs were combed to the side, revealing his twinkly blue eyes. Lexi sighed.

I guess I could sit next to him, she thought. But before she could make her way to the back of the classroom, Jack Yu jumped in front of her and settled next to Jeremy. Kylie continued waving and shouting, "Lexi! Over here!" so she gave up and sunk into the chair next to her.

"Pray class, dost thou knowest why I am dressed in this peculiar fashion?" Juliette began.

Meredith's hand shot up: "You got a part in a play and you're leaving the school?"

Juliette frowned. "Content thee, for my loyalty lies here. Another guess?" She turned to Lexi. "Willst thou venture a guess?"

Lexi gulped. "Um, something to do with Shakespeare… like you said yesterday?" she answered softly.

"Thou speakest true!" she laughed. "Ah, 'the play's the thing'!"

"Yes!" Meredith cheered, pumping her fist in the air. "I love plays. I want to be the lead!"

"Fear thou not, for we shall all have parts to play," said Juliette.

Then she handed out a stack of books. When Jack Yu got his copy, he groaned out loud. "Oh no! Are you serious? This is a mushy girl's play!"

Lexi looked down at the cover: *Romeo and Juliet* by William Shakespeare. When she flipped through the pages, it was as if the characters were speaking a foreign language, talking the same way Juliette was. She could only understand a word here or there. What did *anon* or *wherefore* even mean?

Kylie raised her hand: "Why do they talk like this? I mean, I know it's supposed to take place a long time ago, but so does *Dracula*, and besides the Transylvania accents, they all talk pretty normal."

"Romeo and Juliet takes place in the fourteenth century," explained Juliette. "The language is old. People spoke more formally back then, and Shakespeare created his own words and sounds to make things sound better, funny, or more poetic. Has anyone here ever watched this play performed? Or seen the movie versions?"

Lexi remembered strolling through Central Park with Aunt Dee this summer past the Delacorte Theater where they put on Shakespeare plays outdoors. She shyly raised her hand and Juliette smiled. "Yes, Lexi?"

"I think I saw a statue of them in Central Park outside the Delacorte Theater."

"Yes! Do you remember what they were doing?"

Lexi thought hard. "They were kissing." The class erupted in laughter and her cheeks flushed.

"Calm thee!" Juliette summoned the class back to attention. "Yes, they were kissing. In this play, Romeo and Juliet are star-crossed lovers. That means their relationship is doomed to fail."

Lexi sneaked a glance at Jeremy. She secretly hoped their relationship wasn't doomed to fail before it even began! She wondered if he'd laughed at her kissing comment. But he seemed too busy doodling in his notebook. So he liked to draw too! She knew they had so much in common!

"Starting Thursday, a gentleman from Great Shakes for Kids will be coming to our class to help us learn the play and stage it for a big production on Valentine's Day," Juliette continued. "Some of you will be acting, and others will be helping to build scenery and sew costumes. The entire fifth grade will be involved."

"I hope there's an evil wizard somewhere in here," Kylie whispered to Lexi. She was flipping through the pages and couldn't figure out much of the text either. "Or a monster. Or a witch. I think Shakespeare has some witches…"

But Lexi wasn't paying attention. She was still staring at Jeremy.

"You really like him, don't you?" Kylie whispered, noticing her friend in a trance.

"No!" But she felt awful lying to her friend, so she added softly, "I mean, maybe…"

"I thought so," Kylie replied. "That's great, Lexi!"

Lexi wasn't sure how great it was, but it felt good to finally share her secret with someone. And she was relieved that Kylie didn't make fun of her. She seemed really happy.

"I never had a crush on a boy before, so I'm not sure," Lexi confided. "My Aunt Dee says when you fall for someone, you feel all warm and mushy inside."

"Like a cupcake fresh out of the oven!" Kylie smiled.

Lexi frowned. "I just get so nervous whenever I'm around him. I don't know what to say!"

"Don't worry," Kylie assured her. "We'll think of something."

Baking up a Plan

"Pupcakes? Seriously?" Lexi read the order Jenna had just taken over the phone for a special rush delivery Sunday morning. They had just twenty-four hours to make them.

"This lady is crazy about dogs—she has six of them, all different breeds," explained Jenna. "She wants us to do four dozen cupcakes for a party with different dogs on top, and she'll pay us extra if we can do it on such short notice."

Lexi sighed and whipped out her sketchbook. "We could do a chocolate lab on a devil's food, a pink poodle on a strawberry, a white bichon frise on a vanilla, and maybe a Dalmatian on a chocolate chip?"

Kylie looked over her drawings. "Sounds good. Let's do little chocolate candies for the eyes and nose. I think we have some left in our kitchen cupboard." She was digging past the containers of sprinkles and colored sugar when she saw something that gave her a great idea.

"Lexi, I think I got it!" Kylie exclaimed, placing a small container of red cinnamon candy hearts on the counter.

Lexi looked at it. "You want me to make the dogs' eyes out of red hearts?"

"No! Jeremy!"

"You want her to make Jeremy out of red hearts?" teased Jenna.

"No!" cried Kylie. "This is the way to get Jeremy to like you. Let's bake him cupcakes and you can give it to him with a note: Love, Your Secret Admirer, L.P."

"So it's true? You *do* like Jeremy?" Sadie asked.

Lexi rolled her eyes. Why did Kylie have to bring that up again?

"Come on, *amiga*, your secret is safe with us!" Jenna insisted. "What's the plan for making Jeremy fall head over heels for you?"

Lexi mulled the idea over. If there was anyone she could trust, it was her PLC girls. "Okay, but it doesn't leave this room." She flipped through her sketchbook to the page titled, "Bake Me, I'm Yours." On it, she'd drawn a rich, gooey, dark chocolate cupcake with chocolate frosting and a marshmallow heart on top. "I've always wanted to try this one."

"Wow. That is a really *sweet* cupcake," whistled Jenna. "I don't know anyone who wouldn't love you if you baked that for them."

"Jeremy's chess club meets in the library on Mondays, the same time I have my reading tutor," said Sadie. "Maybe I could leave the cupcake on top of his backpack when he's not looking."

"That's brilliant!" said Kylie. "What do you say, Lex?"

Lexi was afraid of what Jeremy would think. What if he told everyone on the chess team? What if he didn't like her and laughed in her face? What if he thought her braces were ugly—or that she was stupid because she almost never raised her hand? "I don't know, guys…"

Kylie put her arm around Lexi's shoulders. "You know how my dad got my mom to marry him, right?"

"He proposed?"

"Yeah, but he did it with Milk Duds."

"Huh?" asked Lexi. She knew Kylie's dad had a silly sense of humor, but Milk Duds?

"They ate them on their first date when they went to see *Titanic* at the Jupiter Cinema. My dad remembered and spelled out *Marry Me, Jackie* in Milk Duds on my mom's front porch two years later."

"Well, it could have been worse," chuckled Jenna. "He could have proposed on a sinking ship."

Sadie wrinkled her nose. "I'd rather a guy ask me to marry him at a Knicks game, on the JumboTron!"

Lexi thought it over. "Did your mom say yes?"

"Well, eventually…" Kylie hesitated. "She kind of wanted a diamond ring first. But the point is, it was a sweet gesture, and it totally won her heart."

Lexi chewed the eraser on her pencil. "I'll think about it—after we get these four dozen pupcakes done by tomorrow morning."

"Yeah, this is one *ruff* order to fill," giggled Jenna. "You gotta admit it: even after the summer, I still got it!"

☆✦☆

Monday morning, Kylie caught up to Lexi in the auditorium.

"Call me Cupid!" she beamed, handing her a bag of pink, heart-shaped marshmallows. "I found them at the baking supply store in Greenwich. Perfect for Jeremy's cupcake, right?"

Lexi pulled her aside and whispered, "I never said I was baking him a cupcake! And please, be quiet. I don't want anyone to hear!"

"Lex, you have to do something! Jeremy's never going to know you like him unless you make the first move." She handed her the marshmallows. "All the girls are free next Sunday afternoon. And I found a great recipe for gooey brownie cupcakes…"

"I'll think about it," Lexi said. What she really meant was "I won't think about it." Because thinking about Jeremy made her palms get all sweaty and a lump form in her throat.

"You promise?" pleaded Kylie. "You sugar-sweet swear?"

Lexi nodded but crossed her fingers behind her back. It wasn't lying if she did that, right? "I sugar sweet swear with sprinkles on top." That should convince Kylie!

Now all she had to do was convince *herself* to bake Jeremy a delectable cupcake that would speak louder than words.

Where There's a Will
(Shakespeare), There's a Way!

After Juliette's colorful costume, Lexi was sure Mr. Higgins, the founder of Great Shakes for Kids, would show up in a cape and tights—or at the very least waving a sword. Instead, he was dressed in a dark black suit and tie and carried a briefcase.

"My name is Rodney Higgins," he told the class. "I have a doctorate in English Literature from Oxford and studied at the Royal Academy of Dramatic Art in London."

Juliette stifled a yawn. "You want us to call you Dr. Higgins….or Professor Higgins?"

"Mr. Higgins will do just fine," he replied, sounding snippy.

Kylie leaned over and whispered in Lexi's ear, "Wouldn't they make a cute couple?"

That was it—her friend was completely nuts. First Kylie was playing matchmaker for her and Jeremy, and now Juliette and Mr. Higgins?

"I played Romeo on the West End, as well as Macbeth and Hamlet," he added.

Juliette smiled politely. "Really? I've played Juliet, Viola, and Ophelia."

"You don't say," Mr. Higgins replied, completely forgetting the entire class was listening in on their conversation. "And where would that be?"

"At Stratford. I studied at the National Theatre School of Canada."

"I see," Mr. Higgins sniffed. "Well, I think *my* résumé speaks for itself."

Kylie kicked Lexi under the table. "Can't you just see the sparks fly between them?"

Lexi looked at her teacher, then at Mr. Higgins who had turned his back and was now writing with perfect penmanship on the Smart Board. There were no sparks, and there was no way that Juliette would ever fall for him. She was wearing a *Wicked* Broadway show T-shirt and jeans, while Mr. Higgins looked like one of her father's stuffy partners at his law firm.

"Am I boring you?" Mr. Higgins asked, as Juliette yawned again, this time loudly.

"No not at all. I'm fascinated by Shakespeare."

He raised an eyebrow. "Apparently, since you've played all the great roles *in Canada*."

Juliette's face turned almost as red as her hair. "Are you saying I am not as good an actor as *you*?"

Kylie grabbed Lexi's wrist. "This is getting good!" she squealed. "I've never seen Juliette get this mad at anyone—not even me when I accidentally piped green frosting on the teachers' lounge wall!"

Lexi watched as the two teachers had a heated discussion in the corner of the classroom. They tried to keep their voices down, but every so often she caught a word or two...

"Pompous!" "Amateur!" "Nincompoop!"

The last word was Juliette's before she marched to the door and held it open. Mr. Higgins gathered his briefcase and walked out in a huff. The fourth-period bell rang and the class lined up to go to lunch.

"I can't wait to see Jenna and Sadie and tell them about *Rodney and Juliette*," giggled Kylie. "It's so romantic!"

"They hate each other!" Lexi insisted. "She threw him out of the class!"

"A minor setback," replied Kylie. "Did you ever see *Bride of Frankenstein* when she meets Frankenstein? Worst first date ever!"

"I don't think Juliette would appreciate you calling her the bride of Frankenstein," Lexi said. "Or you playing Cupid for her and Mr. Higgins."

But Kylie wouldn't hear of it. As far as she was concerned, love was in the air at Blakely.

"I think I caught Jeremy sneaking a look at you in drama today," she told Lexi.

Lexi sighed. "He doesn't know I'm alive."

Kylie did her best mad scientist impression: "She's alive! She's alive!" and tried to make Lexi laugh. But it was no use. She'd gotten her braces tightened yesterday and it hurt to smile. Besides, she didn't believe Kylie. Every time she tried to make eye contact with Jeremy, he'd look away or hide behind Jack Yu. Once he asked her if he could borrow a pen for a grammar test, but that was the most they'd ever said to each other.

"I think Rodney and Juliette have a better chance than me and Jeremy," Lexi pouted. "Why would Jeremy like me, anyway?"

"Because you're smart, pretty, and really talented," offered Sadie, resting her lunch tray on the cafeteria table. "I wish I could do half the things you can, Lexi."

"You're kidding, right?" asked Lexi. "I wish I could sink a hoop as easily or run as fast as you can, Sadie."

"The point is, everyone at this table is unique and special," Kylie said.

Jenna raised a juice box in the air. "A toast to the girls of PLC!" Then she froze. "Don't look now, but Jeremy's in line for seconds of hot lunch!" She pushed her empty plate at Lexi. "I could go for another helping. Lex, would you mind?"

Lexi gulped. Go stand next to Jeremy in line? She wasn't sure she could will her feet to stand, much less walk in that direction. But before she had a chance to hesitate, Jenna dragged her up and pushed in behind Jeremy.

"Now say something!" she whispered.

Lexi shook her head wildly. "No! I can't!"

"You can!" said Jenna, and with that, she purposely bumped into Jeremy, sending his plate flying in the air and splattering all over the cafeteria floor.

Jenna dashed back to her table, leaving a horrified Lexi staring at the mess of spaghetti and meatballs on the floor.

"I-I-I'm sorry..." she stuttered. She braced herself for Jeremy to yell at her or call her stupid.

Instead, he shrugged. "It's okay. It was an accident...I guess."

They both bent down at the same time to wipe up the spill and smacked foreheads.

"Ow!" yelped Lexi. For a moment she thought she saw stars from the collision. Then again, it might have been because Jeremy was only inches away, looking so adorably apologetic.

"Now I'm sorry!" he said. "I'm a klutz. Are you okay?" He helped Lexi to her feet.

"Fine," she said, picking a strand of spaghetti out of her hair.

Jeremy blotted the marinara sauce off his white T-shirt with a napkin. It reminded her of how Aunt Dee had dribbled Popsicle juice all over her shirt in Central Park and rubbed it in.

"Pretty—looks like tie dye," she said softly.

Jeremy glanced down at the big red stain he was absent-mindedly rubbing in. "Gee, I never thought of it that way…it is kind of cool." He smiled. "Maybe I'll leave it like this—if you think it looks good. I mean, you're an artist, right?"

Lexi blushed. "Um, I guess."

"No, you are! I saw your map of the thirteen colonies hanging in the fifth grade hallway. It's really good!"

He'd checked out her map? He'd noticed it? He'd noticed her? Lexi felt giddy…

"Thanks," was all she could manage.

Jeremy smiled again. He had such perfect white teeth. They sparkled in the cafeteria lights. Lexi ran her tongue across her rainbow-colored braces. He must think my smile is gross! she thought.

"You sure you're okay?" he asked, handing her a clean tray.

Lexi nodded, keeping her lips locked tightly together. "Mm-hmm."

"Okay, then I guess I'll get some more spaghetti and meatballs. It's my favorite."

Walking back to the table, Lexi felt like she was floating on air.

"So you forgive me now?" asked Jenna. "I was waiting for you guys to share a strand of spaghetti and rub noses, like the dogs in *Lady and the Tramp*." She began to hum "Bella Notte."

Lexi came back to her senses. "You shouldn't have done that, Jenna. What if he had gotten really mad?"

"The point is he didn't," Kylie reminded her. "Sometimes guys need a little push. So Jenna gave him one."

"It was actually a big push," Jenna pointed out.

"So now what? Dump chocolate milk on his head?" Sadie chuckled.

"Now we commence with Operation Bake Me, I'm Yours," answered Kylie.

Lexi watched Jeremy scooping more meatballs onto his plate. She noticed a few strands of spaghetti still hanging in his hair and it made her smile. Even covered in cafeteria food he was cute.

"I'm in," she said.

On a Role

After a conference with Ms. Santoochi, the assistant principal, Juliette gave in and allowed Mr. Higgins back in the drama classroom. He was, as Ms. Satnoochi pointed out, an expert on teaching Shakespeare to children. Even if he did have bad manners and a humongous ego!

"I'd like to welcome back Mr. Higgins," she told the class through gritted teeth.

Mr. Higgins took over the Smart Board and began laying out the plot and characters of *Romeo and Juliet*. Lexi's head was spinning from all the diagrams.

"There are so many names! Mercutio, Benvolio, Capulets, Montagues…how are we supposed to keep them all straight?" she asked Kylie.

But Kylie was most interested in the scheming Friar Lawrence character. "I totally want to play him," she told Lexi. "He gives Juliet a potion that makes her appear dead when she's really sleeping. That is so cool. Do you think something like that really exists?"

Lexi shook her head. "The only thing I can figure out is that Romeo and Juliet love each other, but their families are fighting." She looked over again at Jeremy. "I don't know what I'd do if I loved someone and my parents forbid me to see him." She remembered her dad's reaction to her staying with Aunt Dee—he freaked out and tried to convince her mom it was the worst idea in the world. He really didn't like her, and she was a member of the family! What if he hated Jeremy? What if, like Romeo and Juliet, their stars were crossed?

"We'll be announcing the casting at the end of the week," said Juliette.

"What? No auditions?" Meredith protested. "I've been memorizing Juliet's lines already!"

"No, no auditions. We'll go around the room, taking turns reading the different parts aloud. Then Mr. Higgins and I will decide who plays what character and who will be helping with the important work behind the scenes."

"So not fair!" Meredith grumped.

The first reading didn't go very well. Jack Yu and Meredith acted the parts of Capulet and Lady Capulet—husband and wife, and Juliet's parents.

Jack could barely get out a line with a straight face. "How now, kinsman!" he bellowed, slamming his fist on the desk.

"He's yelling in my ear!" complained Meredith. "I refuse to work with amateurs!"

Kylie was next, reading the part of the friar. "Much I fear some ill unlucky thing!" she cackled like an evil, mad scientist and held her pen in the air, pretending it was a knife about to plunge into someone's heart.

"Romeo and Juliet is a romance, not a horror movie," sighed Mr. Higgins. "*Next!*"

Abby and Julia read the nurse and Juliet…and giggled through most of it. "Madame Julia, your mother craves a word with you!" chuckled Abby.

"It's *Juliet* not Julia," Mr. Higgins groaned. "Please stick to the lines on the page."

"Why does Juliet need a nurse?" asked Julia. "Is she sick or something?"

"A nurse is a trusted family servant," explained Mr. Higgins. "Like a baby-sitter. She's cared for her since she was a baby."

"Juliet *still* needs a baby-sitter?" Julia asked.

Abbey read her next line and burst out laughing. "What lamb? What ladybird?" She laughed so hard she fell off her chair. "This play is hilarious!"

Mr. Higgins banged his head against the wall. "All right, who do we have left to read?" He went down the class list, looking for names.

Lexi sunk under her desk. She knew there were only two kids left who hadn't had a turn: her and Jeremy. *Don't call on me, don't call on me...*

"Lexi and Jeremy, you can read Juliet and Romeo's balcony scene!"

Lexi felt like she was going to faint. Read a love scene with Jeremy? How could she? She'd die of embarrassment! She shook her head no and tried to hide behind her script.

Kylie leaned over and whispered in her ear, "Lexi, you can do it!"

She took a deep breath and forced herself to focus on the single page in front of her—not on her giggling classmates, not her teachers or Kylie, not even Jeremy, who was fidgeting uncomfortably in his seat.

"Romeo, Romeo..." she began softly. She pictured herself standing on a balcony in the moonlight, dressed in a flowing, white gown, peering down at Jeremy as he held his arms out to her. The words suddenly made sense: she felt Juliet's pain—she understood how torn she was between her love for Romeo and her love for her family. And when she finished reading, there were tears in her eyes.

"That was excellent, Lexi," said Juliette. "You really connected with your character." Lexi nodded and looked over at Jeremy who gave her a thumbs-up and smiled. She felt her heart do a little skip.

"Okay, guys, that's it for today," said Juliette. "I don't think Mr. Higgins can take much more!"

As the class filed out of the drama room, Lexi hoped Jeremy would hang back to talk to her. No such luck. He raced off with Jack to get to phys ed. Who was she kidding? Jeremy would never love her the way Romeo loved Juliet! He wouldn't recite poetry in the moonlight. He wouldn't even spell it out in Milk Duds.

On Thursday, Mr. Higgins handed out the cast list and script. "I do not want anyone complaining about the casting," Juliette warned.

"Sometimes you get the starring role, and other times

you get the chorus," added Mr. Higgins. "At least that's what I hear. I've always been the star…"

Lexi was hoping that her teachers put her in charge of scenery. She would be great at painting backdrops to look like the bustling streets of Verona.

"No way!" shrieked Meredith, reading the casting list. "I'm the old nurse and Lexi is Juliet?"

Lexi grabbed the yellow sheet of paper on her desk and saw her name at the top of the list. Beneath it was Jeremy's name…as Romeo.

"Oh no," she whispered to Kylie. "This cannot be happening!"

"Woo-hoo! I'm the friar!" Kylie cheered. "I get to poison you!"

"Kylie!" Lexi grabbed her hand. "You're not listening! I'm supposed to stand on a stage and be the star of a play? I'm supposed to kiss Jeremy in front of the entire school? I'll die!"

"Yup," replied Kylie. "Juliet *does* die in the play. So cool! You have to make it look really gory when you plunge the fake dagger into your heart."

Lexi buried her head in her hands. This was the worst thing that had ever happened to her in her entire life.

Even worse than the time she threw up in the middle of her fourth-grade book report! She raised her hand. "Mr. Higgins, I really can't play this part," she pleaded.

"Of course you can," he replied. "You did an excellent job the other day, and I have no doubt you will make a great Juliet." That made Lexi feel a tiny bit better…until she saw Jeremy's face. He looked as scared as she did.

Juliette came over to her desk to offer more encouragement. "Lexi, no one read Juliet the way you did. You totally get her, and I think doing this play will be really good for you. It will help you come out of your shell."

Lexi sighed. She didn't want to come out of her shell. She liked it just fine in there. In fact, she wanted to crawl back in right now, like a turtle, and stay tucked away till the play was over.

Aunt Dee to the Rescue

Lexi tried to forget about the entire day as she piped straw-berry frosting into delicate swirls on a cupcake. A client wanted three dozen that looked like tutus for a ballet re-cital, and they had only a few hours after school to bake and decorate them.

"Don't talk about it," Kylie whispered to Jenna.

"Talk about what?" asked Jenna, popping another tray filled with white chocolate chip batter into the oven.

"You know *what*," whispered Sadie.

"Oh, you mean the play!" Jenna blurted out. The frosting in Lexi's hand squirted up and out of the top of the bag.

"Hmm, my mom's not going to be happy with pink polka dots on the ceiling, but I think it's pretty." Kylie tried to lighten the mood.

"Sorry," Lexi sighed. "I'm just freaking out over this

whole play thing. I can't play Juliet. I'll forget my lines. Or throw up. Or pass out. Or fall off the balcony."

"Well, I'm on scenery, so I'll make sure I build you a nice cushy tree to break your fall," joked Jenna.

"I mean it, guys, I can't do this!" Lexi cried.

"Lex, you say that every time we give you a new cupcake to decorate for an order, and you wow us," said Kylie. "Do I have to remind you about the hedgehog cupcakes?"

Sadie nodded. "The toasted oats and coconut for the spiky fur was pure genius."

"You said you couldn't do that either, and you did," Kylie insisted. "You can do this too. We'll be right there, cheering you on."

"Thanks," said Lexi, picking up her pastry bag again. "But my mind's made up. I'm going to tell Juliette tomorrow that I won't do it. Let her give the role to Meredith or someone else."

"You want someone else kissing Jeremy?" Jenna gasped.

"No. But what choice do I have? Sadie, what about you?"

Sadie looked up. "What about me?"

"You're Lady Capulet. Can't you just switch parts with me?"

Sadie shook her head. "I'm nervous enough having to

memorize all those lines with my dyslexia," she said. "Juliet has twice as many. Sorry, Lexi. No can do!"

That night, Lexi's Aunt Dee called to find out how the first few weeks of school and the cupcake club were going.

"Okay, I guess," Lexi replied.

"Okay? Just okay? Not fantabulous?"

Lexi smiled. She loved how Dee always put two words together to make her own new word, like fantabulous (fantastic and fabulous), splendiful (splendid and wonderful), and gramazing (great and amazing). Shakespeare had nothing on her! Aunt Dee was an original, and people were drawn to her, as Lexi's mom said, "like bees to honey." Lexi wished the same was true for her. Why couldn't she have more confidence and charm? A certain "somethin'-somethin'," her aunt called it. Lexi pictured it as a magical neon sign that sat over your head and flashed, "I'm special! Everyone loves me!" But she was pretty sure if there was any sign over her head it read, "I'm a disaster. Run as fast as you can!"

"Go ahead, I'll TiVo the new episode of *Dancing with the Stars*," said Dee. "Spill!"

Lexi hardly knew where to begin! "Well, first Kylie didn't like my idea for the back-to-school cupcakes, then Jenna was teasing me about liking Jeremy, then I got the lead in the school play, and I have to tell him I love him in front of the entire universe!"

"Is that all?" Aunt Dee laughed. "Girlfriend *and* boyfriend trouble! Lexi, honey, you've got your hands full!"

"I know! What should I do, Aunt Dee?"

"About the boy or the play?"

"Both. I'm supposed to be Juliet and Jeremy is Romeo. I can't go onstage in front of a whole auditorium filled with people!"

"*Can't* is not a word in my vocabulary," Dee replied. "I believe you can do anything you set your mind to. If you asked me a year ago if I could speak Japanese, I would have said, 'No, I can't.' So I took a few courses, and now *watashi wa nihon go wo hanashimasu*!"

"What does that mean?" sighed Lexi.

"It means I speak Japanese and you play Juliet," Dee insisted.

"Fifth grade stinks," said Lexi. "And it's just barely getting started!"

"Honey, fifth grade will be funificent if you just give it

a chance. Besides, you're not going to deprive me of seeing my niece do Shakespeare, are you? I'll be right there in the front row. Just look for the big pink hat."

Lexi giggled. "Thanks, Aunt Dee. You're pretty amazeriffic."

Lexi had to admit she did feel a little better after her aunt's pep talk. Maybe she was blowing this entire *Romeo and Juliet* thing way out of proportion. Maybe it wouldn't be such a big deal. Maybe Jeremy was actually *glad* she was his Juliet. He did give her a thumbs-up, didn't he?

Lexi pulled out her sketchbook and flipped to a page in the middle. There was only one way to tell—and it had a big heart-shaped marshmallow on top.

How Sweet It Is

Lexi inspected the ingredients the girls had gotten for Jeremy's brownie cupcake. "Are you sure this is the best semisweet chocolate? This cupcake has to be fudgilicious," she explained.

"Fudgi*what*?" asked Sadie. "Is that a word?"

"It's an Aunt Dee word," Lexi said. "It means delectably fudgy, like biting into a chocolate dream."

Jenna sampled a corner of a chocolate square. "I read that chocolate contains more than 500 flavors, which makes it more complex than any other food." She offered Lexi a taste.

"I don't want complex. I want yummy," Lexi replied. The Belgian chocolate melted in her mouth.

"Well?" asked Jenna. "Yummy enough for Jeremy?"

"Let's hope so!" Lexi replied. As the girls worked to melt the chocolate and butter together in a small saucepan, Lexi carefully chose the cupcake liners (pink with red hearts) and placed them in the muffin pan.

"How many walnuts do you want?" asked Sadie, chopping them into tiny pieces. "The recipe calls for a cup."

"I think too many nuts will overpower the fudge factor," Kylie answered thoughtfully. "Let's go with three-quarters of a cup."

When she poured the batter in, Lexi saw that it looked dark and glossy. She placed the pan in the oven, set it for exactly twenty minutes, and crossed her fingers. She stared at the oven door.

"We've made brownie cupcakes before," Jenna assured her. "They'll be great."

"They have to be perfect," Lexi said, nibbling her nails. "I want Jeremy to think these are the most delicious cupcakes he's ever tasted."

"Well, they're created by PLC, so they will be," Kylie bragged.

When the timer dinged, Lexi stuck a toothpick in the center of one of the hot cupcakes and checked it. It came out perfectly clean.

"It's ready!" she said, and raced to her box of piping tips to select one.

Kylie beat the dark chocolate frosting until it was creamy and smooth. Jenna stuck a finger in the bowl to take a lick.

"*Dios mío! Muy delicioso!*" she exclaimed. "I don't have any English words to describe how good this is!"

Lexi filled the pastry bag with frosting, then began to expertly pipe a swirl of chocolate on each cooled cupcake. The frosting formed a beautiful ruffle around the edges.

"Gorgeous!" Kylie watched Lexi work her magic. She delicately placed a pink, heart-shaped marshmallow on top of the fluffy peak in the center.

When all twelve cupcakes were done, Lexi looked them over, selecting her favorite and placing it in a red cardboard cupcake box with a clear plastic window. On the lid, she attached a sticky note: "To Jeremy, From Your Secret Admirer, L.P." The girls dug into the rest of the cupcakes.

"Are you sure you don't want to sign your name?" Sadie asked, licking her fingertips. "So he knows for sure who gave him the cupcake?"

Lexi looked nervously at Kylie. "Do I want to?"

Kylie thought for a moment. "No, you should create a little air of mystery, a little suspense. Keep him guessing!"

"This isn't a movie," Lexi said. "I'm not a monster who's going to pop up out of the dark and scare him!"

"You never know," giggled Jenna. "Kylie could probably lend you some fangs and fake blood."

Lexi rolled her eyes. "Guys, this is really important to me." She wanted everything to be just right and was worried her friends were not taking it seriously.

"We know," Sadie assured her. "It's gonna be great. I'll put the cupcake on top of Jeremy's backpack while he's busy playing chess in the library."

"He'll take a bite and have to meet the cupcake baker of his dreams!" Jenna chimed in.

"You think?" Lexi said. She wasn't sure. What if Jeremy thought the cupcake was just okay. What if he didn't care who baked it for him and just gobbled it up because he was hungry after school?

"We'll do the big reveal the next day in drama class," Kylie suggested. "You'll go over to Jeremy and ask, 'Did you like the cupcake?'"

"That's it? That's all I have to say?" Well, that was a big relief! Lexi thought for sure the girls would tell her to recite a Shakespearean love sonnet.

"That's it. The less said, the better," insisted Kylie. "My mom's a great tennis player, and she always says to put the ball in someone else's court. Let him be the one to tell you how he feels."

Lexi nodded. She guessed she could do that.

"And if you freeze up, you can always pass him a note," Jenna suggested. "It's a piece of cake, Lexi. I mean, a piece of cupcake."

The next afternoon, just as planned, Sadie excused herself from her reading tutor in the library to go to the bathroom. She made sure Jeremy was distracted and studying his opponent's move on the chess board before she slipped out the door. Lexi, Sadie, and Jenna were all waiting for her in the hall.

"Here ya go," said Kylie, handing Sadie the red box containing Lexi's cupcake.

"Make sure you don't smush it," Lexi pleaded.

"Have I ever smushed a cupcake?" Sadie asked.

"With or without your skateboard?" Jenna teased.

Sadie turned to face Lexi. "I promise I will not smush it."

She returned to the library and delicately placed the cupcake box on top of Jeremy's green backpack. She hurried back to her tutor but kept a close eye on the clock. Chess club ended at 3:45 p.m. Only fifteen more minutes till Jeremy found his sweet surprise.

Outside the library door, Lexi paced back and forth while Jenna and Kylie peered through the glass window.

"I wonder if he'll eat it right away or take it home and eat it there," Kylie mused.

"Do you think he'll share it with anyone? His chess club friends?" Jenna asked.

"Would you two stop! You're making me a nervous wreck," said Lexi, resting her head against the wall. "The suspense is killing me."

Just then the period bell rang and Lexi jumped.

"Oh my gosh! This is it!" she screamed, grabbing Kylie by the shoulders and shaking her. "He's going to see it!"

All three girls pushed to get a glimpse in the tiny door window.

"I can't see anything!" whined Lexi. "Is he going to his backpack?"

Kylie nodded. "He's walking over right now!"

"I wanna see!" huffed Jenna, pushing the girls out of the way.

"No, I wanna see!" Lexi shoved back.

Just then, the door opened, and all three of them landed in a pile on the library floor.

"What is going on?" asked Ms. Applebaum, the school librarian. "I thought I heard some commotion out here."

"Nothing, nothing," Kylie smiled. "Just waiting for Sadie…"

"Um, hi?" Sadie waved from the other side of the room.

Lexi was at the bottom of the heap, so she couldn't see what Jeremy was doing. But when she got to her feet, she saw he was holding the cupcake box and reading the note.

"Oh my gosh," she swooned. "I feel sick!" Jenna and Kylie grabbed her under both arms and steadied her.

"Stay cool," Jenna whispered. "And whatever you do, do *not* throw up on me!"

Jeremy read the note for a few seconds. His face was expressionless. Then he opened the box and examined the cupcake. Lexi held her breath.

"Let's go, Jeremy," Jack called. "You're coming to my house to play my new video game, right?"

Jeremy was still staring at the cupcake. "Yeah, sure," he answered Jack. Then he tossed the cupcake—note and all—in the trash and walked out of the library.

Lexi wiggled loose from her friends' grip. She stared in horror at the cupcake in the garbage can.

"Maybe he was full...he didn't want a snack?" Sadie tried to soothe her.

"I'm sorry, Lexi," Kylie added. "We thought for sure he'd love it."

"If you ask me, he has no taste," Jenna threw in. "Anyone with taste would love that cupcake."

Lexi was speechless. She felt like a piece of chewing gum, spit out and squashed on the bottom of someone's sneaker.

"Lex, say something," Sadie begged. "You're scaring us."

She looked at her friends, glancing from face to face. "He hates me," she said, tears streaming down her cheeks. The words and feelings now came tumbling out. "He knew it was me. He hates me. He hates everything about me."

"No! That's not true!" Kylie insisted. "It was just a mistake. Maybe he didn't understand what it was?"

"He understood and he threw it away," Lexi sobbed. She bolted out of the library. Kylie wanted to run after her, but Jenna held her back.

"Let her go," she said. "I think she needs to be alone."

"Besides, there's nothing we can do or say to make it better," Sadie sighed. "This is a disaster. Poor Lexi!"

When Lexi got home, she dug out the biggest blank canvas she could find and propped it on her easel. Sadie liked to dribble a ball when she was upset, Jenna ate Oreos, Kylie watched a marathon of mummy movies, but the way she handled disappointment was very simple: she got out her palate and painted the way she was feeling.

She began by blending primary cyan, ultramarine blue, and mars black, till it made a dark, ominous, swirling ocean. Then she dotted it with foamy titanium white to make the waves crash on the beach. Finally, she painted a gray sky with flecks of gold lightning. She stepped back and looked over her artwork: it felt angry, sad, and scared, all at the same time. Lexi sighed. So did she. She was furious for letting Kylie talk her into this whole crazy cupcake plan— and brokenhearted that Jeremy had rejected it and her. She was also terrified to go to school tomorrow. Jeremy would be there. He'd probably have told Jack all about what happened and they'd had a good laugh over it. Lexi dabbed the tears in the corners of her eyes and accidentally smeared blue paint on her cheeks.

Her big sister, Ava, knocked on the door and poked her head inside.

"It's super quiet in here," she remarked, then laughed out loud. "Lexi, you look like you're ready for Camp Echo Pond Color War. Is that blue team paint on your face?"

Lexi scowled. "No. Can you just please leave me alone?"

Ava looked concerned. "Are you okay? What happened?"

The last thing Lexi wanted to do was tell her perfect older sister that she had been tossed in the trash by her first crush.

"Nothing. I just want to be alone with my painting," she replied.

"Okay, but if you need to talk…"

Lexi nodded and went back to painting dark storm clouds. How could Ava—or anyone for that matter—possibly understand how she felt? It was so humiliating! She kept seeing Jeremy throwing her cupcake in the garbage, as if she was hitting the Rewind button on the TV remote.

She heard her computer ding. She had email. It was probably Kylie, trying to make her feel better. *As if…*

Instead, the email was from Great Shakes for Kids. It contained the rehearsal schedule for *Romeo and Juliet*. Lexi groaned and hit Delete. She'd go to school early tomorrow and tell Juliette she was quitting. The less she saw of Jeremy, the better for both of them.

Rodney and Juliette

The next morning, Lexi arrived at school an hour early. She had been up practically all night, tossing and turning, trying to figure out what she would say if Jeremy confronted her. It was a long night and now it was going to be a long day.

"Juliette?" she called, knocking on the drama classroom door. Through the window, she could see there were people inside. She peeked in and could make out Juliette and Mr. Higgins in the back of the classroom. Juliette was standing on a chair and Mr. Higgins was kneeling on one knee. They looked pretty silly—and busy—but Lexi couldn't hear what they were saying. So she pushed the door open a tiny bit more…

"Be but sworn my love," Juliette said, touching a hand to her heart.

"By blessed moon, I vow," Mr. Higgins replied, taking her hand in his. Juliette leaned forward, and they looked deeply into each other's eyes.

Lexi gasped. This looked a little too real to be acting! Could it be…*Rodney and Juliette*? Could Kylie have been right about them? It certainly looked like it! The doorknob creaked loudly in her hand.

"Who goes there?" shouted Mr. Higgins. He put his glasses back on and Juliette hopped off her chair.

"I do," Lexi said tiptoeing into the classroom. "Sorry," she apologized to her teachers. "I just needed to talk to you about the play."

Juliette motioned for Lexi to come take a seat beside her. "We were just figuring out the staging. What's up, Lex?"

Lexi took a deep breath. "I have to quit."

"Why?" Mr. Higgins seemed disappointed. "We thought we'd chosen the perfect Juliet…aside from this Juliette." He looked over at her teacher and winked.

"I just can't, that's all," Lexi continued. "Besides, I don't think Jeremy would want me to."

"Are you two not getting along?" asked Juliette. "But I thought—"

"So did I. I was wrong. He hates me," Lexi replied.

"Sometimes a relationship starts out on the wrong foot," Juliette said. "Maybe it's all a misunderstanding?"

Mr. Higgins nodded. "Ms. Dubois and I initially had a little misunderstanding."

Juliette coughed. "A little? Try humongous!"

"Anyway, we worked together this past week and discovered we have a lot in common," he added. They smiled at each other.

"The point is don't just give up, Lexi," Juliette reminded her. "'The course of true love never does run smooth.'"

"Shakespeare again?" Lexi asked.

"Of course!" Mr. Higgins replied. "The bard knew a thing or two about romance. Just give it a try for a few days and see how it goes between you and Romeo. Fair enough?"

Lexi agreed but felt a knot in the pit of her stomach the moment the class came into the room. Thankfully, Jeremy was late and in a hurry to get to his seat. He didn't have time to say anything to her.

"We're going to break up into small groups today and run lines," Juliette explained. Lexi was supposed to rehearse a scene with the Nurse aka Meredith. Even acting with Meredith would be better than facing Jeremy.

"Find a quiet corner with your partners," Juliette instructed the class. Meredith had already grabbed a spot in the front of the room and was making strange sounds with her mouth.

"Mama made me eat my M&Ms!" she sang. "Sally sells sweaty socks by the seashore!"

"What are you doing?" Lexi asked, puzzled.

"Warm-ups," replied Meredith. "Every actor knows that."

She then began to read her lines in a strange, clipped British accent. Lexi thought she sounded like Mary Poppins.

"Anon! Anon!" Meredith bellowed. "Come, let us away…"

Lexi *wished* she could away!

"A word, ladies," Mr. Higgins interrupted.

"How do you like my accent?" Meredith asked.

Mr. Higgins wrinkled his nose. "Well, dialect is a difficult thing to master. Why don't you try delivering the lines *without* an accent? I think it might be more powerful."

Meredith smiled. "I can do that." It took her almost the entire period to get through the scene. "Don't you think the nurse should say a little more here? She's a very important character in the play!"

Mr. Higgins rubbed his temples. "Yes, yes, every role is important, Meredith," he replied. "But I don't recommend rewriting Shakespeare."

Meredith shrugged. "Whatever."

Lexi was just glad she escaped drama without any drama. She saw that Jeremy was busy rehearsing with Jack who played his enemy, Tybalt. Jack wanted to know when they could practice dueling with swords.

"Tomorrow," Mr. Higgins sighed. "I need to make sure we have a first-aid kit handy."

"*En garde!*" Jack yelled, flourishing his sword in the air. "This is going to be awesome!"

"I also want to do some work on the Romeo and Juliet balcony scene tomorrow," Juliette added. "Lexi, Jeremy, make sure you memorize your lines for homework tonight."

Lexi looked over at Jeremy to see his reaction. He nodded and didn't seem disgusted by the thought of having to rehearse with her. Phew!

☆ ☮ ☆

Kylie caught up to Lexi in the hall. "How did it go?"

"Okay, I guess," Lexi said. "Jeremy didn't say anything about the cupcake catastrophe. And I told Mr. Higgins and Juliette I wouldn't quit the play for a few days."

"Good! That's plenty of time to do some detective work," Kylie exclaimed.

"What kind of detective work?"

"We need to find out *why* Jeremy threw away your cupcake. Jenna thinks maybe he's allergic to nuts or something. She saw him going to the nurse last week."

Lexi thought it over. Well, that would explain why he tossed the cupcake so quickly. "How do we find out?"

"We investigate," Kylie replied. "We can all take turns following Jeremy."

Lexi shook her head. "No way!" The last thing she needed was for Jeremy to spot her spying on him.

"I am an expert at secret intelligence," Kylie insisted. "I've learned from some of the best monster hunters in the movies."

"Like you're an expert at matchmaking?" Lexi pointed out.

"Exactly! Did you see the look Juliette gave Mr. Higgins this morning? She was cracking up at his jokes, and all he said was 'Better three hours too soon than a minute too late.' What's funny about that?"

Lexi wasn't about to fill Kylie in on what she'd seen before class. If Juliette and Mr. Higgins were destined to be a couple, then they didn't need any help.

"I've always wanted to be a junior bridesmaid at a wedding," Kylie gushed. "And can you just imagine the huge white cupcake tower we could make for it? You could sculpt little white doves and a bride and groom out of fondant…"

Lexi couldn't help but chuckle. Kylie had a knack for getting carried away, especially when cupcakes were involved. "I don't think we should start baking those wedding cupcakes just yet," she said.

"You're right. We have to focus on Jeremy first."

Swords and Swoons

Mr. Higgins gave Jack a long list of rules and regulations before they practiced the fight scene.

"Do not aim your sword at anyone's face, is that clear?" he said sternly.

"Yup." Jack nodded. "Can we start now?"

"And every time I lunge forward, you step back. A duel is really a choreographed dance routine. Is that understood?"

"Yeah, yeah, I get it. Can we fight now?" He was getting impatient. "I played a lot of Ninja Reflex on my Wii last night. I'm ready."

"Your sword is a prop, not a weapon. The goal here is to make the scene authentic. Not wound your fellow actors…"

Before Mr. Higgins could finish his speech, Jack charged forward screaming, "Hiyah!"

The boys in the class cheered, "Get him, Jack! Get him!"

"The correct term is *en garde* not *hiyah*," Mr. Higgins

replied, crossing swords with him. With one lightning-quick move, he sent Jack's sword flying from his hand and into the air. It landed with a clank on the floor of the classroom.

"Bravo!" Juliette cheered. Mr. Higgins bowed.

"Awww, you took my sword!" Jack whined. "No fair!"

"All's fair in love and war," Mr. Higgins corrected him. "Next time, you wait till I show you how to use your sword before you try and spear me."

Jack moped but handed his sword back to his teacher.

"Now, speaking of love and war, it's time for the love scene. Jeremy and Lexi, please take your places," said Juliette.

Oh no! Lexi thought. She had prayed the sword fight would take up all of the third period rehearsal and she wouldn't have to practice her scene with Jeremy. No such luck. There were fifteen minutes left.

"Up you go," Juliette said, motioning for her to take her place on the makeshift balcony. Reluctantly, Lexi climbed the step ladder to the top rung and gazed down on Jeremy. He looked as pale and queasy as she felt.

"Okay, Lexi, from the top," Mr. Higgins commanded.

Lexi cleared her throat. She knew the lines, but for some reason her mouth and her brain were not working together. "Um, Romeo, Romeo, art for where—*oh no!*"

Meredith snickered. "I should have been Juliet! She's a disaster!"

"The line is, 'Wherefore art thou?'" Mr. Higgins corrected. "Once again, please."

Lexi took a deep breath and began: "Be but sworn my love…" She looked down at Jeremy who was staring up at her. She imagined him as Romeo, dressed in a blue velvet jacket with gold braiding and buttons. He was so handsome! Suddenly, the room felt like it was spinning, just like the carousel Aunt Dee had taken her on in Central Park. Lexi's knees were wobbling, and the next thing she knew, she lost her balance and toppled off the top step.

"Help!" she squeaked as she fell backward. Jeremy reached up and grabbed her around the waist, gently guiding her down to the floor.

"You okay?" he asked. Juliette and Mr. Higgins had already grabbed her and helped her to a chair. The entire class was gathered around, and Lexi saw that Kylie was right beside her, looking very worried.

"Lexi, you okay?" Jeremy repeated. Lexi nodded. She was so embarrassed, she couldn't answer. She noticed that Jeremy looked worried too—which made her feel a tiny bit better.

"The swoon doesn't come till much later in the play," Mr. Higgins teased. "When she takes the poison. But well done."

"It must have been the ladder," Juliette reassured her. "Makes me dizzy too." She squeezed Lexi's hand. "You'll be okay. The real balcony is a lot less wobbly."

Lexi wasn't sure if it was the ladder, her nerves, or Jeremy's blue eyes that had made her lose her balance.

"What am I going to do?" she whispered to Kylie.

"Like Juliette said, you'll be okay!" her friend attempted to cheer her. But it wasn't helping. She still felt like everything in her life was spinning out of control.

She knew what Aunt Dee would say: "Lexi, honey, you have to face your fears—stare them right in the eye and say, 'Bug off! You don't bother me!'" That's what Dee would do. She wouldn't let a boy or a play or self-doubt hold her back. She'd climb right back up that ladder!

So that's what Lexi did. She got to her feet, turned to Mr. Higgins, and said, "Can I try it again?"

The teachers looked at each other, concerned. "Are you sure?" Juliette asked. "You sure you feel up to it?"

She got to her feet and made her way up to the top rung once more. This time, Kylie stood behind her, spotting her, just in case…

"Romeo, Romeo, wherefore art thou?" she began.

Jeremy blurted out, "I'm right here! I mean, *she speaks!*"

Lexi grinned back. He looked even cuter when he messed up his lines and blushed.

When they were done with the scene, the entire class applauded. "Brava!" Mr. Higgins said. "You do Shakespeare proud."

Shakespeare *and* Aunt Dee would be proud, Lexi thought to herself.

Big Apple Adventure

At the next drama class, Mr. Higgins handed out permission slips for the class to go on a field trip. "I think you'll all enjoy this very much," he said. "Next week, we're going to New York City for the day to attend a matinee of *Romeo and Juliet* at the New York City Ballet."

Meredith jumped up and down. "Yay! I love ballet! I'm so good at it!"

"This is great!" Kylie told Lexi.

"Really? I thought you liked monster movies, not ballets."

"I do! I mean it's great that we can get a whole day to observe Jeremy in action."

Given her dizzy spell in drama class, Lexi had almost forgotten about Kylie's plan to snoop on Jeremy. But Kylie hadn't forgotten! She reminded Lexi of her dog, Poochie, when he got his teeth wrapped around a chew toy. There was no way he would let it go, no matter how hard Lexi tried to pry it out of his mouth. Kylie was not going to let the whole Jeremy thing go either.

"This is an interpretation of *Romeo and Juliet* without any of Shakespeare's words," Mr. Higgins explained. "The story is told solely through dance. It's quite dramatic."

Juliette nodded. "Can you imagine trying to tell a story as complicated as this without any words?"

"I've seen silent monster movies, like *Phantom of the Opera* with Lon Chaney," Kylie volunteered. "There's no talking in that."

"You're right," said Juliette. "You experience the drama through the actors' facial expressions. In ballet, you experience it through the way they move their bodies in dance."

☆ ☮ ☆

On the day of the trip, the entire fifth grade piled into two school buses. Jenna's mom Betty was one of the chaperones. "She's never seen a ballet before and me either!" Jenna said. "I'm so psyched!"

As the bus got off the highway and drove down the Upper West Side of Manhattan, Lexi recognized some of the places her Aunt Dee had taken her over the summer.

"Look!" she said, pointing out the window. "That's Zabar's. They have the yummiest bagels and lox."

"What's lox?" asked Sadie. She was sitting with Kylie, a row behind Lexi and Jenna.

"It's smoked salmon," explained Lexi. "Salty, fishy, and delicious."

Sadie wrinkled her nose. "I don't like anything fishy."

Kylie leaned over their seat and motioned toward Jeremy. "Doesn't *that* look fishy to you?"

Jeremy was digging into a small fanny pack around his waist, popping something into his mouth.

"What's he eating?" Jenna wondered out loud.

Sadie shrugged. "I thought Mr. Higgins said no snacks on the bus?"

"Go find out, Lex," said Kylie. "Pretend you have to ask Juliette something about the play. She's sitting right across from him."

"Why me?" sighed Lexi.

"Because you're up already!" said Jenna, inching her off the seat with her butt. "Out ya go!" Lexi wasn't thrilled, but she made her way down the aisle.

"Uh, Juliette?" she began.

Her teacher looked up. "Lexi, why are you out of your

seat? That's very dangerous! What if we hit a bump or make a short stop?"

Just as she said the words, the bus driver slammed on the brakes to stop for a red light. Lexi went sprawling forward and landed right in Jeremy's lap.

"Hey!" he said, startled.

Juliette helped Lexi to her feet. "This is what I was talking about!" she said. "You could have been seriously hurt!"

"Sorry," Lexi said, embarrassed. She made her way carefully to the back of the bus and her friends.

"Well, that didn't go exactly according to plan," said Kylie.

"I told you I didn't want to do this," Lexi sighed.

"But you did a great job, Lex," said Jenna, picking a few flakes off her shoulders.

"What's that?" asked Sadie.

"Almonds," Jenna replied. "Jeremy must have spilled them on you when you fell on him. Good work!"

"So we know he's not allergic to nuts," Kylie deduced. "Hmmmm…"

"Maybe he didn't have breakfast? Maybe he's starving?" sighed Lexi. "This is ridiculous!"

The bus pulled in at Lincoln Center and the fifth graders lined up around the enormous fountain in the plaza.

"*Qué bonita!*" exclaimed Mrs. Medina. "What a beautiful place this is!"

They walked inside the David Koch Theater and everyone gasped. There were five balconies of red velvet seats and a massive orchestra section. A twinkly globe hung from the ceiling. The stage was wrapped in a gold curtain, and a live orchestra was warming up in the pit.

"We're in the first ring," Mr. Higgins explained. "So we'll have an excellent view of the stage."

"I wish I brought my sketchbook so I could draw this," Lexi said.

"Wait till you see the ballet," Juliette assured her. "It's even more beautiful."

The lights dimmed and a hush fell over the audience. The music by Sergei Prokofiev filled the theater, and the curtain drew back, revealing the vibrant streets of Verona, Italy. Romeo wore pale blue tights and boots and a billowing white shirt. Jack Yu laughed, "You won't catch me wearing tights," but Mr. Higgins shot him a look. When Juliet appeared, she looked as delicate as a dove, flitting around the stage in a flowing white dress and pointe shoes.

"Lexi, you are so lucky to be playing that part!" Jenna whispered.

Lexi agreed—the ballerina was breathtaking, but she couldn't imagine herself ever looking that angelic or graceful. She'd probably fall flat on her face or land in someone's lap—just like she'd done on the bus.

When she appeared on the balcony, Juliet smiled and twirled around on her toes. Then Romeo ran across the stage, a cape flying behind him. Their eyes met and locked on each other. As the music swelled, Romeo drew closer and closer. Juliet descended the stairs, and they began a romantic *pas de deux*. Romeo got down on one knee and lifted Juliet over his head in a graceful arabesque. The dance ended with the lovers' arms wrapped around each other.

When the lights came up for intermission, Mrs. Medina was sobbing. "*Es tan romántico!*" she cried.

"What do you think, Lexi?" Juliette asked.

"I think I'm in big trouble," she said. "I can't do that!"

"You don't have to," Juliette replied. "No pointe shoes, I promise. I wanted you guys to experience this so you could bring more emotion to our version of *Romeo and Juliet.*"

Lexi did feel swept up in the story, especially the second

half of the ballet. In the death scene, Romeo took Juliet in his arms and tried everything he could think of to awaken her. When she wouldn't open her eyes, he thought she was dead and drank poison to end his life as well. Just then, Juliet woke up...too late to save her Romeo.

Lexi poked Jenna. "Do you have a tissue?"

Jenna passed her the box her mom had brought. It was almost empty. "This is heartbreaking!" Jenna cried, blowing her nose.

"*Tan triste! Tan triste!*" Ms. Medina sobbed. "So sad! So sad!"

"Shhhh!" Jeremy hushed them. He was wrapped up in the scene as well.

After the ballet, the fifth grade made its way outside. Everyone took out their lunches and crowded around the fountain.

"We brought Oreos to share," Jenna offered, passing them around with her mom.

All the kids dove in—all except Jeremy, who passed the packages along.

"That's weird. He doesn't like Oreos either?" Kylie remarked.

"Maybe he's a healthy eater?" Sadie suggested. "When

I'm training for a track meet or a big game, I eat lots of fruits and veggies."

"Yeah, but you've never met a cupcake you didn't like," Jenna pointed out.

"And you're on the basketball team and the track team," Kylie added. "Jeremy's on the chess team."

"Maybe he only eats brain food," Sadie said. She was eating a pita stuffed with veggies, humus, and sprouts.

"Chocolate *is* brain food," Jenna pointed out, popping an Oreo in her mouth. "Well, cocoa powder to be specific from the cacao bean. Did you know the ancient Aztecs used to make a breakfast drink out of it to fuel their minds and bodies for the day?"

Kylie laughed. "Jenna, you are like an encyclopedia of chocolate!"

"Maybe you could have given Jeremy a report on how healthy chocolate is before he tossed my cupcake in the garbage," Lexi muttered.

Jenna's mom couldn't help but overhear. "Some people just don't like chocolate," she said. "Jenna's older sister, Gabriella, *no le gusta*."

"That's true," Jenna added. "She likes vanilla ice cream instead of chocolate. I don't get it."

"So Jeremy doesn't like brownie cupcakes but sneaks almonds in his fanny pack. So what?" Lexi complained.

"We're just trying to get some answers, Lex," Kylie said.

"You're just trying to make me feel better that my crush hates my guts."

"That too," Jenna said. "We're your friends. We hate to see you hurting."

"I refuse to believe that Jeremy dumping the cupcake had anything to do with *you*," Kylie insisted.

Lexi closed her lunch bag—she'd lost her appetite. "Well, it's true. Face it, he doesn't like me." She walked away discouraged and climbed back on the bus.

"This is going to take a lot more detective work than I thought," said Kylie, taking a bite of her PB&J sandwich. "That Jeremy is a tough nut to crack!"

14

The Clue in the Cafeteria

Kylie, Sadie, and Jenna all agreed they weren't ready to give up just yet. They'd take turns the next day at school observing Jeremy's every move. Sadie took the first shift. Her mission: tail Jeremy during lunch and recess. Kylie suggested all the girls wear disguises—baseball hats and sunglasses—and report any info immediately.

"He had spaghetti and salad for lunch, no dessert," she briefed the girls. "The pudding parfait looked really good, and he passed."

"What about chocolate milk?" asked Jenna.

"Negative," Sadie replied. "Just a bottle of water."

Jenna was the next shift. Since she had PE with Jeremy, it was easy for her to hide behind the bleachers and eavesdrop on his conversation with Jack.

"You want to come over tomorrow after school? I got the new NBA game for Wii," he said.

"Can't. I have a stupid doctor's appointment," Jeremy answered. "Maybe this weekend?"

Kylie took the last shift—fifth period. Jeremy was in her art class. In the middle of class, he got up and left the room. "Where'd he go?" she whispered to Abby.

"Nurse," she replied. "He goes there a lot."

Kylie knew that Ms. Bayder would excuse her from art class if she pretended to have a paper cut. "It really hurts," she moaned, sucking on her finger. "Can I *please* go to the nurse?" She raced out of the room and down the hall to where Lexi was in math. She knocked softly on the door and interrupted Ms. Nuñez's class.

"I'm sorry. We have an emergency in the teachers' lounge kitchen. Can I borrow Lexi for five minutes?"

Ms. Nuñez pursed her lips and looked suspicious. "What *kind* of emergency?"

"A flood…of frosting…everywhere," Kylie improvised.

"Okay," the teacher said. "Just make it quick and clean it all up before my free period. I don't want to be up to my elbows in frosting."

Kylie yanked Lexi out of the classroom. "How did frosting flood the kitchen?" she asked. "Did Jenna get loose in there again?"

"No, I had to say something so Ms. Nuñez would let you leave. It's Jeremy. He's going to the nurse and I need you to come with me *now*."

Lexi felt her temper start to boil. "Are you serious? You dragged me out of class to help you spy on him? I told you, I won't do it anymore, Kylie."

"Just this once?" she begged her friend. "He looked very serious when he left art, and Abby said he goes to the nurse a lot."

"What does that prove? Maybe he has a headache."

"I don't know. Please just come with me for five minutes?" Lexi knew if she didn't give in, Kylie would continue to whine and plead with her.

"Fine, five minutes," she said, following Kylie to the first floor where the nurse's office was located.

"I'll pretend I'm hurt or something. You stay at the door and listen in," Kylie instructed her.

Lexi crossed her arms over her chest and pouted. This was ridiculous. What could they possibly hope to learn? And what if Nurse Finster realized Kylie was lying? They might get sent to Principal Fontina's office for cutting class! But it was too late. Kylie had already pushed through the door.

"Oh, my stomach," she moaned. "Ow, ow, ow!"

The nurse rushed over. "Where does it hurt, dear?" she asked.

"Here," Kylie pointed to her stomach. "No, kind of here." She pointed to her back. "Well, maybe here." She pointed to her butt. Lexi laughed and covered her mouth so the nurse wouldn't hear. "Oh, it just hurts everywhere!"

"When did it start?" Nurse Finster asked, feeling Kylie's head.

"Um, about a half hour ago."

"Did you eat anything different?"

"No…just a dozen cupcakes." The nurse's mouth dropped open.

"You ate a dozen cupcakes? And that's normal?" she gasped.

"Well, sometimes I eat two dozen. But I was kind of full from lunch." Kylie continued moaning and groaning and rubbing her tummy.

"Well, that's the reason for your bellyache!" the nurse scolded.

"Can I please have a warm compress for my tummy?" Kylie asked sweetly. "Pretty please?"

"Sure. Stay right here." Nurse Finster went to her supply closet. Lexi kept watching Jeremy. He was just sitting there in a chair, not saying a word.

The nurse came back, handed Kylie a hot water bottle, and read a small instrument on the desk next to Jeremy. "Okay, Jeremy, you can go back to class now. Your sugar seems fine," the nurse called. He got up and walked out the door just as Lexi ducked out of sight.

Nurse Finster turned to Kylie. "Now, about you…"

"Gee, I feel all better," Kylie smiled. "I'm good to go."

Nurse Finster stared. "Really? Are you sure?"

Kylie raced out the door. "Yup! I feel great! Thanks!"

When she came out, Lexi was hiding in an empty office waiting for her.

"Did you hear that? Did you hear what Nurse Finster said?" Kylie grabbed her.

"Something about sugar being fine? What does that mean? And if it's fine, then why did he hate my sweet cupcake?"

Kylie considered what they'd overheard. "I don't know. But I know who to ask: your mom."

"My mom is a veterinarian—an animal doctor, not a people doctor," Lexi said.

"But she studied medicine, right? We have a lot of clues. We just need her to help us piece them all together."

After school, Lexi, Kylie, Sadie, and Jenna laid out all the facts for Dr. Poole in her home office while she tended to a cocker spaniel with a splinter in his paw.

"So Jeremy snacks on nuts, doesn't eat any sweets, goes to the nurse a lot, and Nurse Finster told him his sugar was fine?" Lexi's mom repeated the clues back to them.

"That's right," said Lexi. "Does it make sense?"

"It makes perfect sense," said her mom. "It sounds to me like Jeremy may have juvenile diabetes."

Lexi's face grew pale. "What does that mean? He's sick?"

Her mother put the dog back in his carrier and took Lexi's hand. "Well, honey, it's complicated," she began. "Everybody has some amount of sugar, or glucose, in their blood. We couldn't live without it, and glucose comes from the food we eat. But when someone has diabetes, his body has trouble controlling the level of glucose in his blood."

"That sounds really scary," gulped Lexi.

"I'm sure it's hard for Jeremy," Dr. Poole said. "Along with all the things you guys learn in school, he's also had to learn to manage his diabetes."

"And that means *not* eating a sugary cupcake, right?" asked Kylie.

"Probably," said Dr. Poole. "It certainly would explain

why Jeremy doesn't usually eat dessert…or even the best cupcakes in New Fairfield."

Jenna sighed. "I just can't imagine a world without cupcakes! Poor Jeremy!"

"If you want, you can find out more about it," Dr. Poole suggested. She went over to her laptop and called up a website for the Juvenile Diabetes Research Foundation.

For over an hour, the girls pored over the site, reading all the FAQs and stories about kids who were diagnosed with diabetes. "So his body probably can't process sugar," Lexi said.

"And we made him the sweetest cupcake on the planet…major mess up!" groaned Sadie. "No wonder he got rid of it so fast. We're lucky he threw it in the trash and not at us!"

Lexi paged through the site and pondered, "What if we made Jeremy a cupcake he *could* eat?"

"You just said sugar was a no-no," Kylie reminded her.

"'But a rose by any other name would smell as sweet,'" Lexi quoted *Romeo and Juliet*.

"Okay, you lost me," Jenna complained. "Now you want to give him roses?"

"I'm just saying a cupcake by any other name—" Lexi began.

"Is still a cupcake!" Kylie finished her thought. "It

doesn't have to be a sugary cupcake. It can be something savory, like the bakers make with crazy ingredients all the time on that TV show *Cupcake Wars*."

Jenna made a face. "Yuck. They made a tuna cupcake with wasabi cream frosting last week!"

"Spaghetti and meatballs!" Sadie suddenly shouted. "Jeremy gets it anytime it's on the menu for hot lunch. Could we make him a spaghetti and meatball cupcake?"

Lexi pulled her sketchbook and pencils out of her desk drawer. "I don't see why not!" She sketched a cupcake filled with wiggly spaghetti strands, topped with tomato sauce, Parmesan cheese, and a mini meatball.

"Wow!" exclaimed Kylie. "That's amazing, Lex. That's the most creative cupcake I've ever seen!"

Lexi beamed. It was pretty good. She especially liked how the tiny meatball looked like a cherry on top! "And we'll use whole wheat spaghetti, like the American Diabetes Association site recommends." She felt pretty confident that Jeremy wouldn't toss *this* cupcake in the trash.

It took the girls several hours to perfect a recipe. They decided to bake it right in the pan without cupcake liners, and the first version stuck and got burned on the bottom. Plus, the meatballs were a little raw in the center. Lexi's mom offered to help. "You know I make a mean marinara," she laughed, stirring the pot of sauce. The girls rolled the meatballs and let them simmer in the sauce. The aroma of garlic and basil filled the kitchen.

Dr. Poole suggested they coat the muffin pan with non-stick spray, just in case the cheese melted around the edges. This way, the spaghetti slipped out beautifully and formed a neat little cup. The sauce and cheese made a bubbly crust and the meatball was cooked to perfection.

"This is really *pastalicious*," Sadie said. "Did I say that right?"

Lexi laughed. "Yes. I think we can heat it up in the teachers' lounge and give it to Jeremy at lunchtime."

"You sure? You don't want to sneak it to him again?" asked Jenna. "I can always leave it on the bleachers next to him at PE."

Lexi popped a meatball in her mouth. "Nope. I learned my lesson the first time—no more secret admirers. I'm going to make this delivery in person." She sounded sure and confident.

"That's great, Lexi. Good for you!" said Sadie.

Lexi smiled. "Thanks. But maybe you guys can just back me up...in case I chicken out?"

"You mean in case you *meatball* out?" Jenna teased.

"We'll all be right behind you," Kylie said, hugging her. "Always."

15

Special Delivery

Juliette took the tray out of the oven in the teachers' lounge kitchen and placed a piping hot spaghetti and meatball cupcake on a plate.

"Are you sure you want to do this?" she asked Lexi, concerned. "Love is not as simple as following a recipe." Lexi thought her teacher sounded like she was speaking from experience.

"Did you ever have your heart broken, Juliette?" she asked.

"Oh, dozens of times!" Juliette confessed. "My first time was in fifth grade, just like you."

"You had a crush on a boy?" Lexi asked. "What happened?"

"His name was Jean-Paul," Juliette sighed. "He was very tall, dark, and handsome."

"Did you tell him you liked him?"

"Did I! I made him a huge pink cardboard Valentine's Day card covered in hearts and lace doilies."

"What happened?" Lexi sensed there wasn't a happy ending to this story.

"He laughed at me. Right in my face."

Lexi gasped. "That's horrible! That's almost as bad as throwing my cupcake in the garbage!"

"Well, it gets worse," Juliette continued. "He hung it up on the bulletin board outside our classroom. Then *everyone* laughed and made fun of me."

"You must have been so hurt!" Lexi said.

"I was pretty devastated. Then a stuffed pink teddy bear magically made its way into my desk the next day."

"Did Jean-Paul give it to you to apologize?"

"No! It was from Louie!"

Lexi looked puzzled. "Louie? Who's that?"

"The short boy who had a crush on *me*! I thought it was the sweetest gift ever—and forgot all about Jean-Paul."

Lexi considered the story. "Are you telling me to forget all about Jeremy?"

"I'm just saying that hearts sometimes get broken, but they heal pretty quickly."

"What happened to Louie?" Lexi asked.

"Well, it didn't last. I fell for an older man, a sixth grader named Gerard. He had braces and I thought he was very cool."

Juliette handed the plate to Lexi, who dusted the spaghetti cupcake with a thin sprinkling of Parmesan cheese. "Are you ready?"

Lexi nodded. "Ready as I'll ever be."

Lexi marched into the cafeteria where Sadie, Kylie, and Jenna were waiting to back her up. She spotted Jeremy sitting at a table with Jack and some other fifth-grade boys. He looked up as she approached.

Lexi froze in her tracks. "I can't do it," she whispered to her friends. "He's looking at me."

Jenna gave her a gentle push. "Just put the cupcake down in front of him and smile. That's it."

Lexi obeyed, pushing the plate in front of Jeremy.

"What's this?" he asked. But Lexi had already turned and started to run for the cafeteria door. Kylie caught her. "Wait! See what he says!"

Jeremy stared at the plate and the little cup of pasta. "Is this spaghetti and meatballs?"

Lexi was completely tongue-tied. All she could do was nod her head. So Kylie piped up, "Yes! Lexi made it for you. It's a whole wheat spaghetti and meatball cupcake."

Jeremy looked a little uncomfortable.

"Well, we know you usually don't eat sugar…" Lexi said softly. "I wanted to make you a cupcake you *could* eat."

"Oh," he replied.

Jenna gave him a threatening look. "You *better* say you like it."

"Yes! I like her…I mean *it*!" Jeremy blurted out. Sadie, Jenna, and Kylie grinned.

"Well, it was all Lexi's idea," Kylie said.

Jeremy smiled shyly. "It looks really good." He took the meatball off the top and ate it. "It's way better than hot lunch."

Jack tried to grab a forkful. "Lucky!" he whined. "I want one! Lexi, how come you made it just for Jeremy?"

Lexi shrugged. "I thought he would like me…I mean *it*!"

"He does like *you*," Kylie whispered in her ear. "Maybe we should rename our club Peace, Love, and Cupids?"

☆ ☮ ☆

In drama class the next morning, it was time for Lexi and Jeremy to rehearse the final scene of the play. Lexi was both excited and terrified at the same time. She knew all her lines by heart, but she also knew how the scene ended—with a kiss.

"Romeo walks in and sees Juliet's not breathing," Mr.

Higgins directed. "He thinks she's dead and can't live without her." He motioned to the floor. "Lexi, play dead."

Lexi closed her eyes tight and lay down on a floor mat. Jeremy ran his fingers through his hair. "Um, what do I have to do?"

"Just look miserable," Mr. Higgins answered. Lexi opened one eye and peeked: Jeremy was doing a pretty good job of that!

Jeremy took a deep breath and said his line "Oh, my love…" so quietly Lexi could barely hear him.

"What? What was that?" Mr. Higgins asked.

Jeremy gulped and repeated ever so softly, "Oh, my love…"

"Louder!" Mr. Higgins bellowed, waving his arms in the air. He was getting frustrated, and Lexi was worried what he might do to Jeremy if he didn't speak up.

"This is a very tragic scene. Like this…" Mr. Higgins instructed. He suddenly grabbed Juliette to demonstrate. "Oh, my love!" he exclaimed, dipping her backward.

Juliette pretended to swoon and Mr. Higgins continued, "Thus, with a kiss, I die!" Lexi sat up and stared. Were her teachers actually going to *kiss*?

Mr. Higgins planted a peck on Juliette's cheek. She blushed.

"Just like that," he told Jeremy. "Can you handle it?"

Jeremy ran his fingers nervously through his bangs again. "Yeah, I think so." He gave Lexi a kiss on the cheek and said, "Thanks for the spaghetti cupcake."

Lexi sat there positively stunned. She was completely unaware of anything going on around her. All she could hear was her heart beating wildly in her ears. All she could see were Jeremy's dreamy blue eyes.

"No, no, no," Mr. Higgins wrung his hands. "Lexi, you're supposed to be dead. Not grinning from ear to ear! And, Jeremy, that's not the line! There are no cupcakes in *Romeo and Juliet*!"

Juliette jumped in. "Rodney," she began sweetly, touching Mr. Higgins' arm. "It's okay." She winked at Lexi. "Besides, maybe there *should* be cupcakes in Verona."

Now it was Mr. Higgins's turn to blush. "Yes, dear."

"Let's take it again from the top!" Juliette announced. And this time Lexi was happy to oblige!

16

Sweetheart

"I'm worried about all these Valentine's Day orders," Kylie said. The girls had planned on working the entire weekend to make sure every cupcake was ready by Monday, Valentine's Day. They arrived at eight o'clock sharp at Kylie's house Saturday morning, eager to bake.

"My dad and brothers said they'd help us deliver," Sadie said, placing a purple candy heart that read BE MINE on top of a frosted cupcake.

"It's not just that," Kylie explained. "This is turning out to be our biggest holiday yet. We have over 100 orders here."

Jenna did some quick math. "Two hundred thirteen dozen is…2,556 cupcakes. Not to mention the thousand cupcakes we promised Ms. Fontina for the Blakely Valentine's Day party and a thousand for the Golden Spoon."

Lexi was very quiet. She was focused on sketching a

pink peony she planned to pipe on two dozen chocolate-cherry cupcakes.

"I think we need help," Kylie replied. "Even with us working all day today and tomorrow, we'll never be able to bake and frost all these cupcakes. Maybe I could call my friend Delaney from Camp Chicopee—"

Lexi suddenly snapped to attention. "What? You want to ask Delaney to help us? She doesn't know how to bake cupcakes!"

"Well, we'll teach her," Sadie said, carefully measuring a teaspoon of baking powder and adding it to the mixing bowl. "None of us knew how to bake when we started out last year."

Jenna nodded. "Lex, you can't possibly decorate 5,000 cupcakes all by yourself. You need extra hands—we all do."

Lexi was not happy but gave in. "Fine. But if she messes up, I'm saying TYS—told ya so!"

A half hour later, Kylie's doorbell rang. "That's Delaney!" she said racing to get the door.

"Great," Lexi grumbled under her breath. She could hear lots of happy squeals as Kylie reunited with her camp friend.

"They sure sound happy to see each other!" Sadie said.

Kylie brought Delaney into the kitchen to meet PLC. "Jenna, Sadie, Lexi, this is Delaney Noonan."

Lexi glanced up to get a look at the girl Kylie had raved about. She didn't seem anything special: she had long blond hair and braces and wore jeggings and a sweatshirt with a peace sign on it.

"She looks a little like you, Lexi!" Sadie whispered.

"I don't see it!" Lexi sniffed, but she thought the same thing.

Jenna handed Delaney an apron and set her up scooping the batter into the wrapper-lined pans.

"Keep it really neat and no more than two-thirds full," Jenna instructed.

"Yes, sir!" Delaney joked.

Jenna kept a close eye on her. "Not bad, not bad at all!" she said, pleased. "Delaney, you may have a future in cupcakes!"

Kylie smiled. "TYS! Delaney's great at everything she does—remember Color War?"

"OMG, how could I forget! That swimming relay was insane. But we came in first with my butterfly stroke and your backstroke. *Go Blue!*"

Lexi fumed. "Let's try her out on piping." She knew a beginner could never master a pastry bag and tip the first time. She handed Delaney a bag filled with passion-fruit buttercream.

"Do it like this," she commanded, demonstrating a perfect swirl with a peak in the center.

"I think I got it," Delaney replied. She held the bag in her hand and squeezed it expertly with the palm of her hand. It took her seconds to duplicate Lexi's swirl.

"Wow! Impressive!" Jenna whistled. "Delaney, you're a natural."

"Here," said Lexi, shoving a dozen more in front of her. "Make yourself useful." Delaney topped two dozen white chocolate raspberry cupcakes with a vanilla cream cheese frosting, then piped dark chocolate buttercream on three dozen devil's food cupcakes. Kylie showed her how to cut shapes out of fondant with tiny cookie cutters.

"Like this?" Delaney asked, holding up a perfect red heart.

"Exactly!" said Kylie. "You rock!"

Lexi hated that Delaney could handle whatever they threw at her—and was so cheerful about it. She and Kylie sang Lady Gaga songs as they worked.

"This is so much fun!" Delaney exclaimed, putting red lips on some mascarpone whipped frosting. "You're so lucky to have this awesome cupcake club."

"Maybe you could join PLC?" Kylie suggested. Lexi saw that one coming!

"Really?" asked Delaney. "That would be so cool! Then we could hang out all the time!"

Lexi interrupted—she had to change the subject fast. "This next order is for Red Hot cupcakes. What does that mean? We don't have any recipe yet for that."

"I was thinking Red Hot candy hearts on top and a spicy cupcake and frosting," Kylie said.

"We could do a Mexican Chili Chocolate Cupcake," Jenna suggested, "and top it with a cinnamon cream cheese frosting. But we'll need chili powder and ground cayenne pepper."

"We should have all those spices from our family taco nights," said Kylie. "You get working on the batter with Delaney. Sadie and I will tackle the frosting."

Jenna put all the ingredients on the counter. "We want the cupcake to have a kick," she explained. "A pinch of cayenne should do it."

Delaney looked at the small container of orange powder. She gave it a shake into the dry ingredient bowl. "A pinch of cayenne! Check!"

About twenty-five minutes later, the cupcakes emerged from the oven a deep, dark chocolate color. "These look perfect," Jenna observed. She opened one wrapper and took a taste.

"*Dios mío!*" she cried, fanning her tongue. "Water! I need water!"

Sadie raced to get her a glass, and Jenna gulped it down and asked for another…then another.

"That cupcake is way too spicy—my mouth is on fire! Delaney, how much cayenne did you put in there?"

"A pinch, just like you said," Delaney answered.

"A pinch is about one-eighth of a teaspoon," Kylie explained.

"Oh," said Delaney. "I kind of sprinkled in a little more than that. Like maybe three or four tablespoons?"

Jenna was still gulping down water. "Yeah, you sure did!"

Lexi felt bad for Jenna…but she couldn't help chuckling. "I guess Delaney still has a lot to learn about baking cupcakes."

Delaney looked sad and embarrassed. "I'm really sorry. I didn't know."

"It's okay," Kylie said, putting an arm around her friend. "We've all made tons of mistakes. Right, Lexi?"

Lexi shrugged. "I guess," she replied, and went back to decorating.

In seven hours, the girls had managed to bake, decorate, and box half the Valentine's Day orders. They were all covered, head to toe, in flour and frosting.

"This is hard work!" Delaney yawned. "We've been at it all morning and afternoon! I'm exhausted!"

"So I guess you won't be joining PLC," Lexi said hopefully.

"I'd have to think about it," Delaney replied. "I'm on the swim team at my school and we have a lot of weekend swim meets."

"That's okay, Delaney," Kylie answered. "I understand. Maybe you could help us when you're not swimming."

"That would be great!" Delaney untied her apron and handed it to Lexi. "I guess I won't be needing this?"

Lexi felt a little bad. Delaney *had* been very helpful…

"You can keep it…for next time," she said.

"Thanks, Lexi!" Delaney said, suddenly hugging her.

"Yeah, thanks, Lexi." Kylie smiled and walked Delaney out to the door where her mom was waiting to drive her home.

"I guess Delaney wasn't *so* bad," Lexi said helping Jenna and Sadie sweep up the mess of flour, sugar, and candy all over the floor.

"She was super nice," said Sadie.

Jenna agreed. "Kylie does have excellent taste in friends…"

Lexi was too tired to be jealous or angry anymore. Her fingers ached from piping frosting and rolling fondant. And tomorrow they had a ton more work waiting for them; they hadn't even discussed what they'd be making for the Blakely Valentine's Day party.

Since the *Romeo and Juliet* performance was on February 14, Principal Fontina thought it was only fitting that the cast and audience have a Valentine's Day party following the show. She asked PLC if they would make a romantic cupcake display in honor of the event.

When Kylie returned to the kitchen, she immediately took out her notebook and pen. "We need ideas for an amazing cupcake display. Let's have 'em!"

"What do you think of a giant Cupid that shoots cupcakes?" Jenna suggested. "We could launch cupcakes at people as they walk in."

Kylie shook her head. "Cool but messy. We'd have cupcakes flying all over the cafeteria."

"Good point," Jenna said.

"I got it!" exclaimed Sadie. "A giant pair of lips made out of red velvet cupcakes."

Lexi winced. Working on cupcakes all day, she'd almost forgotten about the play. "Please, let's not make anything to remind me of that kiss onstage! I'm nervous enough!"

"Do you have any ideas, Lexi?" Kylie asked.

For once, Lexi was stumped. She had nothing in her sketchbook that was this big or romantic. Then she remembered Juliette's story…

"A giant Valentine's Day card made out of cupcakes! We can create a huge pink heart and trim it with white lace doilies. We can make light pink and dark pink frosted cupcakes and spell out *love* in the dark ones."

Kylie nodded. "I like it. But how do we get the cupcakes to stay on the card?"

"Let's cross that bridge when we come to it," said Sadie. "We better ask my dad to bring his wood and contractor tools and get started on the heart."

While the girls mixed pink buttercream and baked dozens of mini vanilla cupcakes, Mr. Harris used his saw to cut a six-foot tall heart out of plywood.

"Wow," gulped Sadie, coming outside to check. "That is one ginormous heart!"

"Go big or go home, I always say," her dad replied, sweeping up the sawdust on Kylie's front walk. "And now

I'm going home and leaving the baking to the experts." He planted a kiss on Sadie's head. "Later, hon!"

"So now comes the tough part," said Kylie. "How do we get the cupcakes to stick to the heart?"

"We need something super sticky to hold them," Lexi said. "What about honey…or molasses…or cream cheese?"

The girls gathered the ingredients from the kitchen and started to experiment. Each cupcake slid down the heart and landed on the lawn.

"Okay, plan B. We need to think outside the box and outside the kitchen," Jenna said. She handed Lexi a pack of Fun-Tak from her backpack. "Try this."

Lexi took a big piece of the blue goo and rolled it into a ball. She attached it to the bottom of a cupcake wrapper and stuck it to the heart.

At first, it seemed to work, and Jenna patted herself on the back. "My goo is working!"

Then the cupcake suddenly sprang off the wood and landed on Lexi's sneaker.

"Really, Jenna?" She tried to shake the pink frosting off her laces. "If it won't hold longer than five minutes, we are in big trouble."

Lexi thought hard. "When I want to hang my artwork,

I pin it on my bulletin board in my bedroom," she said. "What if we put Styrofoam over the heart and use toothpicks to pin the cupcakes in place?"

"It's worth a try," Kylie replied, and raced downstairs to her basement to get a few pieces of Styrofoam she had left over from last year's science fair project.

The girls asked Mrs. Carson to help them hot-glue the Styrofoam to the heart. Once it dried, Lexi placed a toothpick through the center of an unfrosted cupcake and stuck it to the board. "We'd have to pipe the frosting on top to cover the toothpick," she explained. "But I think this is going to work. We'll need a lot more Styrofoam and toothpicks, and we can set it all up in the cafeteria the morning of the play."

"That's a great idea, Lex," Kylie added. She also thought piping 1,000 mini cupcakes would help take Lexi's mind off the show…and that kiss!

17

On with the Show!

The Blakely auditorium was packed, standing room only, for the fifth-grade production of *Romeo and Juliet*. Lexi's Aunt Dee arrived an hour early to make sure she got a front-row seat.

Lexi peeked out from behind the curtain and saw her pink, floppy hat and purple clogs. It made her smile and calm down…for a moment.

"You're going to be fine," Sadie assured her. She promised Lexi she'd be right behind her if she panicked.

"What if I forget my lines?" Lexi asked.

"You won't!" Sadie assured her. "You've been reciting them all week!"

"Oh, Lex, you look gorgeous!" Kylie exclaimed. Lexi was wearing a blue velvet dress and a blue cap over her long, blond hair.

"You look great too," Lexi managed. Kylie had on a long brown robe and carried a basket of herbs in her hand.

"You think?" she said, twirling around. "I wanted to wear a bald cap, but Juliette said no. I think Friar Lawrence would look more villainous if he were bald."

"Places! Places!" Mr. Higgins called suddenly. "Five minutes till curtain!" Lexi felt a chill race up her spine. This was it! There was no turning back now!

Juliette placed her hands on Lexi's shoulders. "Put everything out of your mind," she advised her. "You're Juliet, not Lexi. Just go with it."

The first scenes went flawlessly. Meredith threw in a slight British accent now and then as the nurse, and the audience loved when she boomed, "Good MAHROW, good gentleMAHN!" and curtsied. Jack Yu was also a sensation as Tybalt, leaping around the streets of Verona, brandishing his sword in the fight scene. He didn't even mind wearing tights, as long as he got to yell, "Romeo! Thou art a villain!" and chase Jeremy around the stage.

Kylie convinced Mr. Higgins to let her play Friar Lawrence with a hint of dastardly flair. "These violent delights have violent ends!" she said…then cackled mischievously.

As the play unfolded, Lexi was actually amazed at how easily the words came to her. It felt a little like she was running on autopilot. She pretended she was just rehearsing once again in the drama classroom. There was no audience, just her and her classmates reading the lines.

Then in Act Four, came the death scene…and the kiss.

"Remember to lie very still," Juliette instructed her in the wings. "Don't move a muscle."

Lexi nodded. She just hoped her knees wouldn't knock together too loudly!

"Here lies Juliet," Jeremy began. Then he drank from a small red bottle in his pocket. "With a kiss, I die…" He bent over and kissed Lexi's cheek. She tried hard not to smile. It kind of tickled. The "poison" worked, and Jeremy collapsed to the ground. The audience broke into thunderous applause.

Now it was time for Lexi to wake up and see her beloved Romeo dead at her side.

She stood up and cried, "My Romeo!" Then she glanced out at the audience. They were silent, waiting for her to make the next move. There were *so many people*! Where did they all come from? And everyone was watching *her*! Lexi froze. She couldn't remember what came next. Not a word, not a syllable! She knew in the back of her mind Juliet was supposed to die too—but she couldn't move.

"Oh no!" Kylie whispered to Jenna. "This is not good!"

"We have to do something!" Sadie said.

"The dagger! Get the dagger out of Romeo's belt!" Mr. Higgins called to Lexi from backstage.

Lexi just kept staring at the crowd.

Kylie thought quickly. "Can you get me one of the extra pink cupcakes we baked?" Jenna nodded and raced backstage, grabbing one out of a box. She handed it to Kylie.

Cupcake in hand, Kylie tiptoed across the stage. She cleared her throat.

"Fair, Juliet!" she began improvising. "Do not be frightened…"

Mr. Higgins gasped. "Oh no! What are they doing? That's not Shakespeare!"

Juliette hushed him. "I think I know…and it's *brilliant*!"

Kylie reached Lexi and tried to distract her. "I bring you a poisoned cupcake so that you can be with your love, Romeo," she continued.

Lexi still didn't bat an eyelash.

"Take the cupcake and eat it," Kylie said through clenched teeth. "Lexi! Snap out of it!"

Lexi took the cupcake—but said nothing.

"The poison will be swift!" Kylie said, pushing it toward her face. "Take a bite…*now*!"

Lexi nodded and took a lick of the pink frosting.

"Now *die*!" Kylie said, exasperated, giving her a little push.

Lexi fell down onstage.

"Oh, thank goodness!" Mr. Higgins sighed. He was mopping his brow with a hanky.

The audience cheered.

"Drop the curtain! Fast!" Juliette called.

Sadie and Jenna raced over to Lexi.

"Are you okay? Say something!" Sadie pleaded, shaking her.

"Lexi?" said a quiet voice. It was Jeremy and he was holding her hand.

Lexi opened her eyes. "What happened? Why do I have frosting on my nose?"

Kylie laughed. "Death by cupcake!"

Love Is in the Air

At the cast after-party, everyone was raving about the fifth grade's "sweet new twist" on *Romeo and Juliet.*

"What a clever way to make it more relatable to the children," Principal Fontina told Mr. Higgins.

"Yes, well, what can I say?" he boasted. "That's my job."

"Modest as always, Rodney!" Juliette chuckled.

Everyone was gobbling up the pink "poison" cupcakes PLC had baked for the festivities. It was one of PLC's most impressive displays, and Juliette especially loved it. "What would Jean-Paul say?" she teased Lexi. "It's amazing!"

"There's the star of the show!" Aunt Dee cried, scooping Lexi up in a huge bear hug. "You were fantabulous, kiddo!"

Lexi shook her head. "I was awful. I couldn't move. I felt like my feet were nailed to the stage—like the cupcakes we toothpicked to the heart!"

"Well, nobody could tell," Dee insisted. "You looked grief-stricken…just like Juliet. And the cupcake twist? Every Shakespeare play I've ever seen was really boring. But not this one!"

Lexi made her way over to her friends. "Thanks, guys. You saved me."

"Actually, we *killed* you," Kylie pointed out. "It was really cool!"

"Thanks for that too," said Lexi. She spied Jeremy across the cafeteria, surrounded by his family.

"Jeremy must think I'm an idiot!" Lexi sighed. "I almost ruined the whole play!"

"I think you're about to find out," said Jenna. "He's coming this way."

"Hide me!" screamed Lexi. She ducked behind her friends.

"Lexi?" asked Jeremy. The girls stepped aside. "Can I talk to you?"

Lexi bit her lip. "Um, I guess." They made their way over to a quiet table in the corner.

"Your cupcake display is amazing," Jeremy began. "You're such a great artist."

"Thanks," Lexi replied, looking down at her feet.

"And you did a really great job in the play today."

Lexi looked up. "Are you serious? I was terrible! I couldn't say my lines! I couldn't move!"

"Neither could I!" confided Jeremy. "I wanted to reach out and toss you the dagger, but I was so scared, I couldn't move either."

"You were?" Lexi replied.

"Are you kidding? My teeth were chattering, I was so nervous. Especially for the kiss."

Lexi giggled. "I just thought you were cold!"

"Anyway, I got you this." Jeremy took a small box out of his pocket and handed it to her. It was tied with a purple ribbon—her favorite color.

"What's this?" Lexi asked.

"Open it!"

She tore off the ribbon and opened the box. Inside was a silver charm bracelet with three charms dangling from it: a peace sign, a heart, and a cupcake.

"You get it? Peace, Love, and Cupcakes," Jeremy said.

"I love it," sighed Lexi. "It's beautiful!"

Jeremy smiled. "Happy Valentine's Day, Juliet."

"Happy Valentine's Day, Romeo," said Lexi, kissing him on the cheek.

"Yes!" screamed a voice from under their table. It was Kylie.

Lexi peered under the seat and saw her BFF hiding.

"Kylie? Really?" Lexi groaned.

Kylie covered her mouth. "Oopsies!"

"You're lucky to have friends who care about you," said Jeremy. "Nice job in the nurse's office."

Kylie climbed out from under the table. "How did you know?"

"I have my spies too," Jeremy replied.

Suddenly, Jack Yu appeared from behind a column. "Yo!" he said.

Kylie looked impressed. "I never saw you there!" she told Jack.

"I've got serious detective skills," he informed her. "You should see me on Spy Games on Wii. I've broken every high score."

"Do you have Monster Hunter Four?" Kylie asked. She'd been dying to try that game.

"You bet! It's awesome. Wanna come over after school and play it?"

Before she could answer, Lexi accepted the invitation for her. "She'd love to!"

Kylie looked surprised...but happy. "What are friends for?" Lexi winked.

☆ ☮ ☆

It was amazing, thought Lexi, how love truly was in the air at Blakely. She had Jeremy, Kylie had Jack, Juliette had Mr. Higgins, and now, even Aunt Dee seemed to have been struck by Cupid's arrow!

"Oh, Mr. Reidy, you're so smart!" she was cooing at Lexi's science teacher.

"You like science?" he asked Lexi's aunt.

"Oh, yes! I'm thinking of majoring in it next semester at NYU! Maybe you could help me with my homework?"

Lexi noticed that Mr. Higgins was dressed down for the occasion: no suit today, just a bright red T-shirt that said "Give My Regards to Broadway!"

"Juliette bought it for me," he said, noting Lexi's stare. "I rather like it."

"I rather like it too," Juliette said, sneaking up behind him and giving him a hug.

Lexi smiled. Everyone got exactly what they wanted for Valentine's Day. And all it took was Shakespeare…and cupcakes.

Lexi's "Bake Me, I'm Yours" Chewy Chocolate Cupcakes with Chocolate Frosting

Chocolate Cupcake

Makes 12

   6 tablespoons unsalted butter

   6 ounces bittersweet chocolate, cut into ¼ inch pieces

   2 eggs

   ½ cup sugar

   ½ cup firmly packed dark brown sugar

   1 teaspoon vanilla

   ¼ teaspoon salt

   ½ cup flour

   cupcake liners

Directions

1. Preheat oven to 350°F. Place twelve cupcake liners in a cupcake pan.

2. Pour enough water into a four-quart saucepan so that it reaches a depth of one inch. Bring to a boil and reduce heat to low.

3. Combine butter and chocolate in a medium bowl.

4. Set bowl over saucepan. Cook, stirring until melted and smooth, for about five minutes. Remove from heat and set aside.

5. Whisk together eggs in a large bowl.

6. Add sugar, brown sugar, vanilla, and salt. Whisk to combine.

7. Stir in chocolate mixture and then fold in flour.

8. Pour batter into lined cupcake pans.

9. Bake until a toothpick inserted into the center of each cupcake comes out clean, about fifteen to twenty minutes.

Chocolate Butter Cream Frosting

Makes 1½ cups frosting

1 stick unsalted butter at room temperature

2 cups of confectioner's sugar

a pinch of salt

2 teaspoons vanilla

1 tablespoon milk or heavy cream

4 ounces bittersweet or semisweet chocolate, melted and cooled

Directions

1. Beat the butter until smooth by using an electric mixer if desired.

2. Add confectioner's sugar and salt. Beat until most of the sugar is moistened, scraping down the sides of the bowl once or twice.

3. When the mixture is fully combined, add vanilla, milk, and melted chocolate.

4. Increase speed and beat until light and fluffy, about four minutes.

Jeremy's Pastalicious Cupcakes

Spaghetti Cupcakes

Makes 6

- 1 cup tomato sauce
- 4 ounces ricotta cheese
- 3 ounces Parmesan cheese
- 8 ounces shredded mozzarella
- 1 tablespoon milk
- 1 egg
- 1 package pre-cooked whole wheat spaghetti
- 1 package of turkey meatballs (optional)

Directions

1. Preheat oven to 375°F. Spray muffin tin with cooking spray.

2. In a large bowl, mix together the tomato sauce, ricotta cheese, Parmesan cheese, shredded mozzarella cheese, 1 tablespoon of milk, and 1 egg.

3. Pour the cooked spaghetti into the bowl with the tomato sauce cheese mixture. Toss the spaghetti in the mixture, making sure to coat all of the noodles.

4. Add spoonfuls of the mixture into greased muffin tins. It can come up to just below the top of each opening. Press down so the noodles are packed into muffin tin—they will fall apart if not packed enough.

5. If desired, dip the turkey meatballs in tomato sauce and add to the top of cupcakes. Sprinkle with Parmesan cheese.

6. Bake for eighteen to twenty-two minutes.

7. Let cool for a few minutes to set. Run a butter knife around each one to loosen.

Valentine's Day Raspberry Cupcakes with Pink Raspberry Buttercream Frosting

Raspberry Cupcakes
Makes 12

- 1 pint of raspberries, reserve 12 for cupcakes
- 2 teaspoons of lemon juice
- ¾ cup + 3 tablespoons sugar
- 1 stick butter, at room temperature
- 2 large eggs
- 1 teaspoon vanilla
- ¾ cup all-purpose flour
- ¾ cup cake flour
- 1½ teaspoon baking powder
- ¼ teaspoon salt
- ½ cup milk

Directions

1. Preheat oven to 350°F. Line the muffin pan.
2. In a small bowl, smash the raspberries with the lemon juice and 1 tablespoon sugar. Strain and set aside.

3. Mix the butter and remaining sugar together until light and fluffy. (If using an electric mixer, cream for three to four minutes and scrape down the sides of the bowl as needed.)

4. Add the eggs, one at a time, and the vanilla.

5. In a separate bowl, whisk together flours, baking powder, and salt. Set aside.

6. Add the flour mixture to the butter and sugar mixture in three parts, alternating with the milk and beginning and ending with the flour. Beat until combined after each addition.

7. Add in the raspberry mixture. Mix until combined.

8. Fill lined muffin pans ⅔ full with cupcake batter. Place a raspberry in the center of each cupcake.

9. Bake for twenty to twenty-five minutes. Use a toothpick to test for doneness.

10. Transfer pans to a wire rack to cool. It's very important not to leave warm cupcakes in the pan or the cupcakes will become soggy.

Pink Raspberry Buttercream Frosting

Makes 1½ cups frosting

½ pint of raspberries

1 teaspoon lemon juice

2 cups + ½ tablespoon confectioner's sugar

1 stick unsalted butter, at room temperature

a pinch of salt

2 teaspoons vanilla

1 tablespoon milk or heavy cream

red food coloring

Directions

1. In a small bowl, smash the raspberries with the lemon juice and ½ tablespoon sugar. Strain and set aside.

2. Beat the butter until smooth using an electric mixer if desired.

3. Add the confectioner's sugar and salt. Beat until most of the sugar is moistened, scraping down the sides of the bowl once or twice.

4. When the mixture is fully combined, add the vanilla and the milk.

5. Add the raspberry mixture and a drop of food coloring.

6. Increase speed and beat until light and fluffy.

7. Frost Raspberry Cupcakes.

Recipes developed by Jessi Walter, CEO and Chief Bud at Taste Buds Kitchen (www.tastebudskitchen.com).

Carrie's Tips for Saying "I Love You" with Cupcakes

Cupcakes are a sweet way to express how you feel about family and friends. You don't even have to wait till Valentine's Day to do it!

1. Think about the person: What do they like? What are their fave flavors, colors, and hobbies? Bake a cupcake that is as special and unique as they are! For example, if your sis likes pink and takes ballet, why not bake her a pink berry cupcake and top it with ballet slippers made from fondant? If you don't want to make your own toppers, you can find lots of fun ones in all shapes at craft and cooking stores. Or simply print out a pic on your home computer, glue it to card stock, and attach it with a small piece of tape to a toothpick. Instant cupcake decoration!

2. Spell it out! I love to make mini cupcakes topped with simple fondant letters. You can use mini cookie cutters that come in alphabet letters to punch out your

message. Use one letter per cupcake, then make your display on a platter or tabletop. Spell out, *"Love You!"* *"XOXO,"* or even *"You Rock!"*

3. Gift a goodie. Pack a cupcake in a pretty cardboard box or plastic food container topped with a bow. You can give it (like Lexi) to your secret crush or save it for a special occasion or holiday. Home-baked gifts are the best. They show you took the time to make them and really care!

4. Use heart-shaped muffin pans to bake cupcakes. You can find inexpensive ones in cooking and craft stores or even on Amazon (www.amazon.com). If they're silicon, you'll have no problem popping out your cupcake. If the pan is metal, coat first with nonstick spray, then bake and frost. Use a little gel icing to write a message on the heart. I love writing "text messages" on mine: UR GR8, 4EVR, QT, etc.

5. Serve someone a cupcake in bed! I love doing this for my parents on Mother's or Father's Day. Plate a pretty cupcake you've bought or made and serve it on a tray with a glass of milk and a card for the occasion. It's a sweet way to show how much you appreciate them and that you realize they need a little R&R!

6. Send a DIY cupcake kit! Use plastic zipper bags to pack all the dry ingredients (flour, sugar, sprinkles, baking soda, etc.). Type or write up the recipe, and include pretty cupcake wrappers, decorative cupcake picks, even piping bags, and tips if you want to be fancy! Then send your kit to someone for a special day celebration. Baking cupcakes is as much fun as eating them!

For more cupcake news, reviews, recipes, and tips, check out Carrie's website: www.carriescupcakecritique .shutterfly.com and Facebook page: www.facebook.com/ PLCCupcakeClub. You can also email her at carrieplcclub@ aol.com.

For more information about Juvenile Diabetes, check out these websites:

- www.kids.jdrf.org
- www.jdrf.org
- www.childrenwithdiabetes.com
- www.diabetes.org

You can also make a donation to the Juvenile Diabetes Research Foundation at www.jdrf.org.

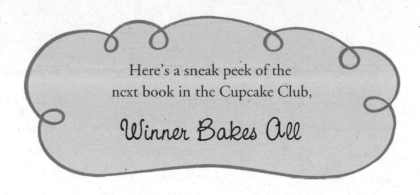

Here's a sneak peek of the
next book in the Cupcake Club,

Winner Bakes All

*Kylie, Lexi, Jenna, and Sadie are about to encounter their big-
gest baking challenge ever! They're invited as one of four bakeries
to compete in Connecticut's* Battle of the Bakers *on TV! Their
mission: come up with a cupcake that combines two ingredients that don't traditionally go together. Taste and presentation
count for major points, and the two finalists will each have to
create a 500 cupcake display. The winner takes all: a $5,000
check and the* Battle of the Bakers *Champion title. Competing
against Peace, Love, and Cupcakes are the state's most presti-
gious bakeries: the sisters of Connecticut Cupcake, Sugar Fingers
Vegan Bakery, and the "Cake King" himself, Benny Bolero...*

"OMG!" cried Lexi. "That Benny guy has won every Food
Network competition he's ever been in. He's a pro! He
built a replica of the *Titanic* out of cake and sunk it in a
swimming pool!"

Jenna nodded. "Seriously, how can we ever expect to win against him?"

Kylie glanced across the kitchen set: Benny was signing autographs for the cameramen. He had commercial mixers, a fondant roller machine, about 100 different types of piping tips. Okay, maybe they were up against some stiff competition. But she would *not* admit defeat before they even began the battle. "He may have more experience, but we have style!" She smiled at her cupcake club friends.

"That's right," their advisor, Juliette, insisted. "You girls have come a long way and you're going to give these bakers a good fight."

Kylie shook her head. "But how? Every one of them is a pro! We're just a bunch of fifth graders." She watched as the Connecticut Cupcake sisters, Cece and Chloe, unpacked their ingredients. They were so organized. Even the pink bows in their hair coordinated.

"Sometimes the least likely person steals the ball," Sadie pointed out. She had played in dozens of basketball competitions and she knew a thing or two about what made a champion. She had a shelf full of trophies at home to prove it. "I was once up against this *giant* girl from Rye Country Day School. I swear she was twelve years old and about six feet tall! Everyone thought she was unbeatable. Well, I faked her out and won the game. We creamed those Rye Reptiles!"

"And we'll cream that Benny Bolero dude," Jenna piped up. "What's he got that we don't?"

"A hit TV show, a chain of bakeries, about a dozen cookbooks with his name on them…" Delaney sighed. "I think he even has a street named after him in Stamford."

"Oh," Jenna sighed. "Good point."

Jerry Wolcott, host of *Battle of the Bakers*, suddenly summoned everyone to attention. There was no more time for nerves or self-doubt. "Cupcake bakers, may I please have one representative from each team in the center of the kitchen?" he called.

Benny strolled over, looking confident. Cece stepped forward after she and Chloe thumb wrestled for it. Kylie looked at Sadie. "You go," she said. "Sadie, you're a real competitor—you know what it takes to win. You're our best bet."

Sadie gulped. "But, Kylie, you're the club president. You should be the leader. Besides, what if they give us something to read? What about my dyslexia?"

Jenna gave her a little push. "Come on, chica, you can do it. Put on your game face and get out there!"

Lexi gave her hand a squeeze. "We believe in you, Sadie."

Sadie walked slowly to the middle of the room where the other three bakers were gathered, awaiting instructions. She stood next to Dina Pinkerton, Sugar Fingers owner and two-time *Battle of the Bakers* winner. Dina was adjusting her apron and looked as cool as a cucumber. Sadie nibbled her nails.

"Hey." Dina smiled. "I've heard some great things about your cupcakes."

Sadie smiled back timidly. "Thanks."

"You nervous?" Dina asked.

Sadie thought about what her basketball coach had told her a million times: "Don't let the other team see you sweat."

"Um, no, not at all," Sadie lied. "I'm cool." She wasn't sure who she was trying to convince, Dina or herself.

"Good!" Dina replied. "Because I'm a wreck! I am before every competition. But adrenaline is a good thing, you know?"

"It is?"

"Sure! Just try to focus on taste, texture, and presentation and keep an eye on the clock. And whatever you do, don't put Maraschino cherries in your cupcakes."

"Why?" Sadie asked puzzled.

"Because the head judge, Fiero Boulangerie, *hates* them. You'll lose if you do—trust me!"

Sadie smiled. "Thanks for the tip!"

"I've got another tip for you," whispered Benny. "Make sure your cupcakes have some zip and zing…if you know what I mean."

Sadie scratched her head. "Um, no, I don't know what you mean."

"A little extra excitement—something that takes it over the top," Benny explained.

"Oh!" said Sadie. "Like the time you made a Fourth of July cupcake on *The Cupcake King* show and it exploded?"

Cece rolled her eyes. "You don't have to throw in all those splashy tricks," she advised. "Just make sure your cupcakes are moist and you use the best ingredients."

Sadie tried to take it all in: zip and zing, no cherries, best ingredients. Her mind was spinning!

"Places! Places, everyone!" Jerry summoned them. "No more talking. I'd like to introduce you to the judges and then we'll start filming."

Three people walked into the kitchen set: Fiero, Carly Nielson, owner of Jimmies, the world's first cupcakery, and…

Sadie's mouth hit the floor. No! It couldn't be!

"I'm sure you know *Battle of the Bakers*' two famous judges, Fiero and Carly," Jerry said. "And our guest judge today is Mrs. Lila Vanderwall, president of the New Fairfield Art Society."

Sadie looked over her shoulder at her fellow PLC members—they looked as shocked and sick to their stomachs as she felt.

"What's wrong?" Delaney whispered.

"Big *problema*!" Jenna gulped. "Mrs. Vanderwall hates Peace, Love, and Cupcakes! We messed up her order."

"Messed up is putting it mildly," Kylie added. "We almost caused an epic art society fail."

"Relax," Juliette tried to reassure them. "I'm sure Mrs. Vanderwall has long forgotten the coat of arms mishap."

Just then, a shriek arose from the judging table: "You! I know you!" Mrs. Vanderwall was pointing an accusing finger at Sadie. "You destroyed my event!"

Sadie tried to keep her guard up. "It was an accident," she said softly. "Bygones?"

The other bakers looked stunned—they'd never seen a judge get this angry *before* she tasted a cupcake.

Jerry tried to calm her down by doing a magic trick: he

pulled a quarter out of her ear. "Hey, Mrs. V.—look at that! Ears to you!" Fiero and Carly chuckled.

But Mrs. Vanderwall was not amused. "I do not like magic tricks," she sniffed. "I do not like puns and I do not like bakers who are unprofessional." She settled into her seat and continued to glare at Sadie.

"Okay…someone needs a little sugar to sweeten her attitude!" Jerry joked. "So let's give it to her. Bakers, here are the rules." He handed a packet of papers to each of the team leaders. Sadie flipped through and tried to focus—it had so many words! Page after page of regulations, diagrams, and legal terms. Each round appeared to be a different challenge ending with the cupcake presentation—if you made it that far.

Dina raised her hand. "Um, could you cut to the chase and just tell us the challenge for Round 1?"

Sadie heaved a sigh of relief. *Yes! Please just tell us what we have to do!*

"Simple," replied Jerry. "The first round requires you to make a cupcake that will wow our judges." He pointed to the table piled high with ingredients in the corner. "But here's the fun part: you must use two ingredients—one from section A and one from section B—that don't go together. This challenge is called the Perfect Pair."

Sadie stared at the table: in section A, there was there were tons of snack foods like potato chips, popcorn, peanut butter, granola, and a mountain of jelly beans. In section B, there were fruits, veggies, hot peppers, even a jar of pickles.

"Holy cannoli!" Benny cried, mopping his brow. "What are we supposed to do with that?"

"That's for you to bake and for us to partake!" Jerry chirped. He pointed to the giant digital clock on the back wall of the studio. "And your time starts *now!*"

Sadie raced back to her team. "What do we want from the table? What can we bake?"

"It's all so yucky," Jenna said. "None of those things go together!"

"Think out of the box, you guys," Kylie pleaded. "There has to be something!"

"What if we do a chocolate–potato chip cupcake?" asked Delaney.

"Way too safe," said Lexi. "This is *Battle of the Bakers*. They want creativity. They want to see something that's never been done before. I've watched every episode, trust me—we need to take a big risk."

"How about popcorn and papaya? Or pickles and Pop Tarts?" Kylie suggested.

"Ew, ew, ew!" Jenna insisted. "This has to be yummy or we're heading home in round 1."

Sadie was the only one not tossing out suggestions. She was too busy looking at the ingredients table, her mind racing a million miles a minute.

"Guys," she said softly. "I think I know what to make."

The girls stopped bickering.

"What?" Kylie asked. "Tell us! We only have 55 minutes left!"

"My parents are the perfect pair—even though they argue all the time. They belong together."

"We know you're worried about your folks getting divorced," Jenna said. "But what does this have to do with cupcakes?"

"Let's do the two foods my parents like combined in a cupcake. That way we won't just win, but maybe they'll see what a perfect pair *they* are and won't break up?"

The girls were all quiet. "It's a great idea, Sadie," Kylie said, putting her arm around her friend. "But what are their two favorite foods?"

"That's the tricky part," Sadie said. "They really don't go together—but I think we can pull it off." She whispered in Kylie's ear.

"Oh no. Really?" Kylie sighed. "Okay, let's put it to a quick vote: all in favor of a chili and cheesecake cupcake, raise your hand."

Jenna gasped. "Chili and cheesecake? *Un momento, por favor!* How spicy are we talking?"

"Hot. My dad likes his chili very, very hot. Like three-alarm-blaze hot."

"Ouch!" said Delaney. "We want to wow the judges…not set them on fire."

"I think we can do it," Kylie interrupted. "A sweet, light cream cheese frosting would balance out the heat of the cupcake."

Jenna nodded. "We could blend some chili spices into a dark chocolate batter. My *abuela* made a delicious 'hot chocolate' cake once. I think I remember how…some cayenne, a little ground chili pepper…"

"And I can make a realistic chili pepper out of fondant and put it on top of the cupcake," Lexi offered.

Sadie cheered. "I knew we could pull it off!"

"Not so fast, ladies," Juliette reminded them. "We haven't pulled it off yet. And the clock is down to forty-five minutes."

"Cupcake bakers, opposites attract…but will you repel the judges?" Jerry teased. "Forty-five minutes left!"

"Team PLC," Sadie said, pulling them all into a huddle just like she'd seen her coach do. "Two-four-six-eight, let's get baking something great!"

Acknowledgments

Thanks so much to everyone who has cheered us on with cupcakes and kindness!

Our loving family: the Kahns, Berks, and Saperstones. A special shout-out to Aunt Debbie Kahn: like Lexi, you're a true artist (and we love you!).

Our *amazing* recipe developer, Jessi Walter of Taste Buds. A spaghetti and meatball cupcake? No problem!

The dedicated staff of PS 6, especially Ms. Fein and Ms. Levenherz for all your help with Book Two! Thank you for the Shakespeare crash course! Hugs and sprinkles to Ms. Fontana (aka Principal Fontina), Ms. Nuñez, Ms. Underwood, Ms. Hoffman, Ms. Cordeira, Coach Rick, and all of Carrie's fellow peer mediators.

Carrie's brilliant teachers at Ballet Academy East: Elizabeth, Olga, Darla, Cynthia, Joseph, Ari, Anne; plus Julia Dubno, all the 2012 Level 2-ers, and the gang at

Dances Patrelle. You all inspire Carrie with your grace and strength! The *Romeo and Juliet* ballet chapter is for you guys!

Carrie's best gal pals: Darby Dutter, Jaimie Ludwig, Abby Johnson, Ava Nobandegani, Sadie and Lila Goldstein, Liyah Lopez, and Delaney Hannon. The boys deserve a big thank-you too: David Ruff (the most hilarious person I know!) and Kyle Rothstein (so glad we met in kindergarten!).

Sheryl's supporting cast: Holly Russell, Kathy Passero, Stacy Polsky, Pam Kaplan, Michele Alfano, Debbie Skolnik. Ladies, I don't know what I'd do without you all!

The cupcake experts who have been so supportive of Carrie's Cupcake Critique: Katherine Kallinis and Sophie LaMontagne of *DC Cupcakes*; Cake Boss Buddy Valastro; and Rachel and Nichelle of *Cupcakes Take the Cake* blogspot.

The folks at Sourcebooks Jabberwocky—we couldn't ask for a better team to work with! Steve Geck, Derry Wilkens, Leah Hultenschmidt, Aubrey Poole, Kelly Barrales-Saylor, and Kristin Zelazko.

Illustrator extraordinaire Julia Denos, for bringing the PLC characters to life on every cover. We dream it, you draw it!

Our agents at the Literary Group: Frank Weimann, Katherine Latshaw, and Elyse Tanzillo.